'They want a family values. They Cormac interjected, **'because I told them I was newly married and looking forward to having a family.'**

Lizzie's mouth dropped open. 'But...that's not true...'

'It is,' he replied, with a faint, feral smile, 'for the purposes of this weekend.'

Lizzie blinked. Her stomach dipped, dropped. She wanted to make sense of what Cormac was saying, yet she had the odd feeling that if she put two and two together she'd get about twenty. Cormac was gazing at her steadily, coldly, his expression like a vice on her mind. Her soul.

'So...how...?' She shook her head, licked her lips. 'What are you trying to tell me?' she finally asked, and her voice came out in little more than a scratchy whisper.

'I'm telling you,' Cormac replied with icy precision, 'that this weekend you're not my secretary. You're my wife.'

Kate Hewitt discovered her first Mills & Boon® romance on a trip to England when she was thirteen, and she's continued to read them ever since. She wrote her first story at the age of five, simply because her older brother had written one and she thought she could do it too. That story was one sentence long—fortunately they've become a bit more detailed as she's grown older. She has written plays, short stories, and magazine serials for many years, but writing romance remains her first love. Besides writing, she enjoys reading, travelling, and learning to knit. After marrying the man of her dreams—her older brother's childhood friend—she lived in England for six years, and now resides in Connecticut with her husband, her three young children, and the possibility of one day getting a dog.

Kate loves to hear from readers—you can contact her through her website, www.kate-hewitt.com

Recent titles by the same author:

THE ITALIAN'S CHOSEN WIFE
THE GREEK TYCOON'S CONVENIENT BRIDE

RUTHLESS BOSS, HIRED WIFE

BY
KATE HEWITT

MILLS & BOON™
Pure reading pleasure

All the characters in this book have no existence outside the imagination of the author, and have no relation whatsoever to anyone bearing the same name or names. They are not even distantly inspired by any individual known or unknown to the author, and all the incidents are pure invention.

First published in Great Britain 2008
Harlequin Mills & Boon Limited,
Eton House, 18-24 Paradise Road, Richmond, Surrey TW9 1SR

© Kate Hewitt 2008

ISBN: 978 0 263 86439 7

Set in Times Roman 10 on 10½ pt
01-0608-56874

Printed and bound in Spain
by Litografia Rosés, S.A., Barcelona

RUTHLESS BOSS, HIRED WIFE

*For Caroline and Ellen,
the two spunkiest heroines I know*

CHAPTER ONE

CORMAC DOUGLAS needed a wife. Tomorrow. Irritation and impatience thrummed through him in time with the drumming of his fingers on his desk. Outside, the crenellated turrets of Edinburgh Castle were shrouded in a thick and gloomy October fog.

He needed a wife. How? Who?

The women he knew were not wife material. Beauties to be seduced or aspiring socialites to be avoided. No one who would be suitable to act as his wife, weekend engagement only.

No one he could entice, bribe or blackmail. Bend to his will.

His narrowed hazel gaze scanned his office—a large, spare room on the top floor of a restored building on Cowgate. He'd gutted the place when he'd bought it five years ago, turned the old, poky rooms into a wide-open space filled with light and exposed brick.

Normally the sight of the office he owned and the memories it banished gave him a satisfaction that replaced his usual restless discontent.

Now it just seemed to mock him. He had the perfect commission, ripe for the taking, meant to be his, and he wouldn't get it unless he had a wife.

The conversation a few days ago with an architect colleague replayed in his mind.

'The Hassells finally want to develop a resort in Sint Rimbert,' Eric had said. 'Something eco-friendly and luxurious, aimed particularly at families.'

'Families,' Cormac repeated without any intonation.

'Yes, they claim it's a needed niche in the market—luxury for the little ones.' He chuckled. 'It's a plum commission.'

'Indeed.'

'I'd go for it myself, but they want to start work in the new year and I'm already booked.' He paused, laughing ruefully. 'I'm also out of the running for another reason—I'm not married.'

'Married?' Cormac's voice turned sharp. 'What the hell does that have to do with anything?'

'Apparently the Hassells are a close-knit family. They want someone dependable to design this resort, with family values, seeing as it's a family resort. Preferably a married man. Of course, that's just the word on the street—they'd never say as much officially.'

'Of course.' Cormac injected a dry note into his voice. 'Presumably that's why I haven't heard of it.'

'Exactly,' Eric agreed, laughing. 'You're not on the short-list, Cormac.'

'Not yet.'

'What are you thinking of? A trip to Gretna Green?'

Cormac knew Eric was joking so he chuckled along with him. 'Not a bad idea.'

'You know your own reputation,' Eric said with a careless laugh. 'But I didn't think you were quite *that* ruthless.'

After the telephone call Cormac had spent a long time staring out at the gloomy skies, the crawl of cars intent on avoiding the traffic of the Old Town.

He imagined the short-list Jan Hassell would have compiled: smug married architects with their happy home lives and uninspired designs.

It was absurd that the Hassells wanted a married man to design the resort. Family values had no effect—at least no positive effect—on one's work. He should know. His work was his life, his breath. And as for family…

He stifled a curse, one hand balling into a frustrated fist. He wanted that commission. It was a fantastic opportunity, but it was more than that. It was a chance to prove who he was…and who he wasn't.

He was the best man for the job, *could* be the best man if given the chance, if he grabbed it.

He wasn't married.

A few hours after the call from Eric, Cormac had made some calls of his own and finally connected with Jan Hassell. After faxing his CV and some designs to Jan, he'd been invited to a weekend house party on Sint Rimbert, along with two other architects. It was a stone's throw from complete success and now all he needed was a wife on his arm, an ornament to prove he had all those damn family values.

To get the commission.

To seize it.

He glanced at some letters on his desk which his secretary had left for him to sign and irritably pulled them towards him. He was just scrawling his name on the bottom of the first page when he stopped. Smiled.

Considered.

He had the perfect idea. The perfect wife.

She just didn't know it yet.

'I'm glad you're doing so well, Dani,' Lizzie said into the phone. She swallowed past the lump which had risen suddenly—stupidly—in her throat. It was ridiculous to feel sad. Dani was happy, enjoying life at university, doing all the things an eighteen-year-old should do.

This was what she'd always wanted for her sister. Always.

There was a low rumble of male laughter from the end of the line and Dani said, 'I ought to go, some friends are coming over…'

'It's only five o'clock,' Lizzie found herself protesting, aware of the prissy censure in her voice.

'It's Thursday, Lizzie!' Dani laughed. 'Weekends at university always start early.' Another male laugh sounded in the background and she asked a bit guiltily, 'Do you have plans for the weekend? Your first weekend alone!'

'Yes.' Lizzie tried to inject some enthusiasm into her voice and failed. 'Yes, I'm going to…' Her mind went blank. Read a book. Take a bath. Go to bed.

'Paint the town red?' If there was any mockery in Dani's voice, it was gentle, but it still stung. 'You should go for it, Lizzie. You've spent too much of your life looking after me as it is. Seize life! Or at least a man.' She giggled. 'Anyway, someone's calling me, so I'd better go…' Giggling again, at someone other than Lizzie, she hung up the phone.

Seize life. Dani's reckless advice rang in Lizzie's ears as she replaced the receiver. It was easy for her sister to seize things; she was carefree, young, thoughtless. She didn't have responsibilities, concerns, *bills* weighing her down.

Lizzie sighed. She didn't want to think badly of Dani. Hadn't she worked so hard—sacrificed her own dreams—so Dani could have hers?

And now she had them. Lizzie knew she should be thrilled.

And she was. She *was*.

Determinedly, she rose from her desk. Perhaps she would paint the town, if not red, then a light pink. She could go to a wine bar on Rose Street, see if anyone from work was going… There was an associate architect she vaguely fancied—John something. Of course, he didn't even know her name.

No one did.

And even as these plans half-formed in her mind, Lizzie knew she would never carry them out. Didn't know how. Didn't dare.

Sighing, she reached for her handbag. She'd make sure her boss didn't need anything else from her tonight and then she'd go home. Alone. Lonely.

As always.

She knocked lightly on Cormac Douglas's door.

'Come in.'

The barked-out command made Lizzie stiffen slightly. Cormac Douglas was in the Edinburgh office for only one week out of four, and she found she preferred the other three. His terse commands were taken better by e-mail or a short note left on her desk than face to face.

Lizzie pushed the door open. 'Mr Douglas? I was just going to head out unless you need me…?'

Cormac stood by the window, hands shoved deep into his trouser pockets, his gaze studying the grey cityscape stretched out before him. 'Need you?' he repeated as if considering the question. He turned to face her, his eyes sweeping her form in a strangely assessing way. 'As a matter of fact, I do.'

'All right.' Lizzie waited for instructions. She was used to staying late when Cormac was in town, although she'd finished all the work he'd given her. Something must have come up.

'Do you have a current passport?' he asked, and Lizzie blinked, nonplussed.

'Yes…'

'Good.' He paused and Lizzie had the feeling he was considering what to say. An odd thought, since Cormac Douglas was the kind of man who *always* knew what to say. 'I have a business engagement,' he finally explained tersely, 'and I need a secretary to accompany me.'

'Very well.' Lizzie nodded, as if this was something she'd done before. In the two years she'd worked for Douglas Architectural Designs, she'd never accompanied Cormac anywhere, not even to a local work site. He preferred to do things on his own. Besides, he was more likely to take one of his assistants from the London office with him than Lizzie, a plain, parochial Edinburgh girl. 'Where are we going?'

'We leave for the Dutch Antilles tomorrow evening and return on Monday. It's a very important commission.' He paused, eyes narrowed, brow furrowed in concentration. 'Do you understand?'

'Yes.' Lizzie's mind was spinning, although she strove to look unruffled. The Dutch Antilles… If her geography wasn't too far off, that was in the Caribbean and at least eight hours by plane. If Cormac was travelling that far simply to court a commission, it had to be serious. And so did she.

She swallowed, heard the audible gulp, and forced herself to meet Cormac's harsh gaze.

'Is there anything I can do to arrange the travel?'

'Yes, book the tickets.' He pushed a piece of paper across the desk. 'The information's there. I'll be out of the office tomorrow, so I'll meet you at the airport, first-class lounge. Just text me the relevant information.'

Lizzie nodded, used to such terse commands. She picked up the paper and scanned the few scrawled details.

She could hardly pump Cormac for information, or ask him what kind of clothes she should bring. Or why he had chosen to bring *her*.

She swallowed down her curiosity and smiled stiffly. 'Is that all?'

His gaze swept over her once more and a strange sardonic smile curved his mouth. Lizzie had the eerie feeling she'd somehow done something that Cormac had expected…and it was a disappointment.

'That's it,' he said and, sitting down at his desk, turned back to his work, dismissing her from both his presence and his mind.

Lizzie slipped silently from the room.

Back at her desk she sank into her chair, her knees weak.

She was going to the Caribbean. She pictured white sandy beaches, tropical forests, tropical *drinks*. People, laughter, sultry breezes. For a moment she allowed a thrill to trickle through her like quicksilver, awakening nerves, dreams, even desires she hadn't known she still had.

Who knew what could happen? Who she might meet?

She had plans for this weekend. Big ones.

After making the necessary travel arrangements, Lizzie got up and shrugged on her coat.

She was going to the Caribbean…*with Cormac Douglas*.

For a moment she paused, her coat halfway on, as she considered what a trip with her boss would be like. Together on a plane, in a hotel, on the beach.

Would Cormac soften in a new, more relaxed environment? Or would he be just as tense and short with her as always?

She pictured him for a moment, tried to imagine his face in a smile rather than a scowl, eyes crinkled with laughter rather than narrowed in scorn. It was virtually impossible. She wasn't sure she'd ever seen Cormac Douglas smile—a kind smile rather than something born of contempt or cold-blooded business acumen.

She gave herself a mental shake; she had no place imagining what Cormac would be like. It didn't matter. All he wanted her for was to take notes, carry papers. And do it well.

And yet…the Caribbean. With Cormac. Another thrill racked her like a shiver—illicit, dangerous. Real.

A fine misting drizzle was falling when Lizzie left work, heading into the busy nightlife of the Old Town.

A few of the other secretaries from the office had invited her out when she'd first started working there, but she'd never been able to go because of Dani.

Now they no longer asked.

Lizzie shrugged this off; caring for Dani was enough, had always been enough.

Except now she was gone.

The last three days had been strange, still, silent. Lizzie accepted it with pragmatic determination, told herself she needed time to develop her own friends and pastimes, things she'd never had time to have before. Time to find a life.

And it would start by jet-setting off to the Caribbean.

A giggle escaped her, a breathless sound of pure feminine fun.

Three days in Sint Rimbert… Anything seemed possible. She was doing what Dani had told her to do. Seizing life.

Even if she had to go with Cormac Douglas, at least she would be getting out, meeting people, having a bit of an adventure.

It was a start…of something.

She left the lights, misty through the rain, of Princes Street and headed towards her house in Stockbridge, a short walk from Edinburgh's Old Town.

The Georgian town house was in an area that had become affluent and cosmopolitan, and as always Lizzie was aware how shabby and run-down her house looked among the others—a weed among roses. It needed new windows, a coat of paint and a dozen other things, as well. None of them were within her budget, but it was home, a house full of memories she wanted to keep.

She unlocked the door and pushed it open, entering the dim hallway. As she had been since Dani's departure, Lizzie was conscious of the silence, the emptiness, the blank spaces.

'Empty nest syndrome at twenty-eight,' she murmured, annoyed with herself. Defiantly she turned on the radio in the kitchen, glanced in the cupboards to see what she could make for a meal and then headed upstairs to change.

He had a wife. Cormac knew he would have to tread carefully. It was a delicate business, maintaining a deceit.

Still, he thought he knew how to play his secretary. Intimidation was the key to someone like her. He shook his head in contemptuous dismissal.

Miss Chandler was one of those unfortunate people in life whose only purpose was to be used.

Use or be used.

Cormac chose the former. Always.

Despite the satisfaction he felt at obtaining his so-called wife, he also felt a restless surging, an uneasy energy pulsing through him. There were too many variables, possibilities. Not everything was under his control. Yet.

Would his secretary be convincing as his wife? He hadn't told her just what was required of her; he'd do it on the plane when there was no exit. No escape.

His mouth curved in a knowing smile. He didn't think she'd balk, but if necessary he could offer her money. No one turned down cold, hard cash.

God knew she could probably use a little extra, even though he considered the salaries he offered to his staff to be generous enough. She wore the same black suit to work every day, clearly something inexpensive off the high street. With her lack of make-up and pale, neat hair, she could certainly use a makeover, or at least some good advice.

Makeover… The word, the thought stilled him. He pictured her showing up tomorrow with a cheap suitcase full of plain, inexpensive little outfits. A secretary's clothes. Not a wife's.

Not *his* wife's.

A possibility he hadn't considered. It would be dealt with. Now.

With a muffled curse, he grabbed his coat and headed outside.

She'd turned the radio up loud so at first she didn't hear the knocking. Not until it become a fierce, methodical pounding.

Lizzie put down the chopping knife, turned down the radio and headed for the door with her heart leaping into her throat.

Who knocked like that? Police or drunks came to mind. She peered out of the hall's narrow windowpane and gasped in surprise when she saw who it was.

She had her answer. Cormac Douglas knocked like that.

What on earth was he doing here? She'd never seen him outside the office…or the tabloid newspapers.

Taking a deep breath, she ran a hand over her hair, which tumbled loosely over her shoulders, and opened the door.

'Mr Douglas?' She eyed him uncertainly, for he looked as grim as ever, his forehead drawn into a frown, his eyebrows an unyielding scowl. He was still a handsome man, she acknowledged, as she had since the first day he'd hired her. Tall, his chocolate-brown hair misted with rain, clear hazel eyes glinting with impatience, his cheekbones high and chiselled, slashed with colour.

'I need to speak with you. May I come in?'

She nodded, conscious suddenly of her own mussed hair, the jeans and white T-shirt she'd changed into. She touched her cheek and realised a dab of tomato sauce had smeared there.

'Yes, of course.'

The hall of her parents' house was long, narrow and high, yet Cormac seemed to fill the gloomy space. He glanced around, and Lizzie knew he was taking in the old, shabby furnishings.

Just then she heard a sizzling sound from the kitchen and, with a murmured excuse, hurried to it.

The tomato sauce was bubbling ominously on the stove and she lowered the gas flame before turning around.

She gave a little gasp of surprise; Cormac stood in the doorway, taking in the pathetic little scene in one cursory sweep of his contemptuous gaze.

Lizzie found herself flushing. She could just imagine what Cormac was thinking. Thursday night and she was home alone, making a sad little meal for one, the radio her only company.

'I'm sorry. I was just making some dinner,' she explained stiltedly. Jazz music played tinnily from the radio and she snapped it off. 'Do you…do you want some?'

Cormac simply stared, raising one eyebrow in silent, scornful disbelief. Lizzie bit her lip, flushing again. Of course he must already have dinner arrangements at some chic restaurant, a far cry from here. From her.

According to the tabloids—as well as the voicemail messages that were occasionally left on the office machine—she knew he was with a different woman nearly every time he was seen, usually at a nightclub or high-class restaurant.

So why was he with *her* tonight? Here?

'Sorry,' she muttered, not really sure why she was apologising. 'Anyway…may I take your coat?'

Cormac was still looking at her, sizing her up in a way she wasn't used to. Lizzie tried not to fidget. He'd never really looked at her before, she realised. She was simply someone to bring papers, answer telephones. Now he was watching her, eyes narrowed, seeming as if he was deciding whether she passed or failed.

Passed or failed *what*?

His hands were thrust deep into his pockets and the shoulders of his overcoat were damp, his hair mussed from the rain.

'All right.' He shrugged his coat off and handed it to her. 'Put that away and then I need to talk to you.'

Lizzie nodded stiffly, feeling like a maid in her own home. She went to hang his coat in the hall. A faint tang of cedar and soap wafted from it and Lizzie felt a strange tingling in her chest, a tightening she didn't really like or understand.

She didn't know this man, she realised. At all. And she had no idea what he was doing here. What could he possibly want to talk about?

Back in the kitchen, Cormac stood in the same place. He was completely still yet he radiated energy, impatience.

His hard hazel gaze snapped back to her with a cold, precise determination as soon as she entered the kitchen.

'I forgot to mention some salient details regarding our trip.' He paused, raking his fingers through his damp hair. 'I'm travelling to Sint Rimbert to court an important commission. Jan Hassell, who owns most of the island, has finally decided to build a luxury resort. It's important to him, of course, that the architect he chooses presents the right…appearance.' He paused, looking at her as if he expected a reply, but Lizzie was baffled.

'Yes, I see,' she said after a moment, although she didn't really.

Cormac let out an impatient breath. 'Do you? Then perhaps you realise that I can't have a secretary who gets her clothes from the rag basket.'

Colour surged into Lizzie's face. It was galling to realise that he didn't think she possessed the proper clothes for such a trip. Even worse was the realisation that undoubtedly she didn't. She swallowed. 'Perhaps you could tell me what I need to bring,' she said with as much dignity as she could muster.

Cormac shook his head. 'I can guarantee, sweetheart, that you don't have it.'

Lizzie lifted her chin. He'd never called her sweetheart before, and she didn't like the casual, callous endearment. 'If I'm not stylish enough for you,' she said shortly, 'there are other secretaries from the Edinburgh office who could oblige you.'

'I'm sure there are,' Cormac returned, 'but I want you.'

He spoke flatly, yet Lizzie felt a *frisson* of awareness, excitement, at his words. *I want you.*

Because of your typing speed, idiot, she told herself. And obviously not her style or appearance. Anyway, she reminded herself, the last thing she wanted was a man like Cormac Douglas to turn his attention towards her. Working for him was difficult enough.

'Well, then,' she finally said, a brisk note entering her voice, 'I'll do my best to look smart. Was there anything else you needed to discuss with me, Mr Douglas?'

'You should call me Cormac,' he replied abruptly, and Lizzie simply stared.

'Why?' she asked after a moment, and he gave her a cool look which spoke volumes about what he thought of her audacity in questioning him.

'Because I said so.'

'Fine.' She swallowed any indignation she felt. It was pointless. Cormac Douglas was her boss and he could do what he liked. Even in her own house. 'Is that all?' she finally got out in a voice of strangled politeness.

'No.' Cormac continued to stare at her, his gaze narrowed and uncomfortably assessing. On the stove the pot of tomato sauce bubbled resentfully.

After a moment he sighed impatiently and, without another word, he turned on his heel and headed for the stairs.

Lizzie's mouth dropped open. 'Just where do you think you're going?'

'Upstairs.'

She followed him up the steep, narrow stairs, unable to believe that he was invading her home, her privacy, in such a blatant and unapologetic way. Yet why should she be surprised? She knew well enough how Cormac Douglas operated. She'd just never been on the receiving end of it before.

She'd never been important enough to merit more than a single scornful glance and a few barked-out instructions. Now her clothes, her home, her whole *self* were up for scrutiny.

Why?

Cormac strode down the hallway, poking in a few bedrooms, mostly unused and shrouded in dust-sheets.

'This place is a mausoleum,' he remarked with casual disdain as he closed the door to her parents' old bedroom. 'Why do you live here?'

'This is my *home*,' Lizzie snapped. Her voice wavered and she stood in front of him, blocking his way down the hall towards her bedroom. 'What are you doing here, *Cormac*? Besides being unbelievably nosy and rude.' A disconnected part of her brain could hardly credit that she was speaking this way to her boss. Another part was surprisingly glad. She glared at him.

'Seeing if you have appropriate clothes,' Cormac replied. 'Now, move.'

He elbowed past her none too gently and Lizzie was forced to follow, grinding her teeth as Cormac strode into her bedroom and looked around.

Her bed was rumpled and unmade, her pyjamas still on the floor, along with a discarded bra and blouse. The stack of paperback romances by the bed suddenly seemed revealing, although of what Lizzie couldn't even say.

She didn't want Cormac here, looking over the detritus, the dross of her life. It wasn't fair. It wasn't right.

It was incredibly uncomfortable.

He glanced around once, taking in every salient detail with narrowed eyes, a smile of complete contempt curling one lip, before he strode to her wardrobe and flung open the doors.

Lizzie watched with a growing sense of incredulity, irritation and shame as he thumbed through her paltry rack of clothes, mostly sensible skirts and dresses, a few different blouses to go with her black suit. There had never been any need for anything else.

'As I thought,' he said with an aggravating note of cruel satisfaction. 'Nothing remotely suitable.'

'I'm your secretary,' Lizzie snapped. 'I hardly think you'll lose this commission because I'm not dressed like—like one of your tarty girlfriends!'

Cormac swivelled slowly to face her, light beginning to gleam in his eyes. 'What would you know about my girlfriends, tarty or otherwise?'

Lizzie swallowed and shrugged defiantly. 'Only what I see in the tabloids.'

He laughed softly. 'You believe that tripe? You *read* it?'

'You *do* it,' Lizzie snapped back, goaded beyond all sense of caution.

'Do I?' He took a step forward, his voice dangerously soft. 'Is *that* what you're after?'

'What I'm after,' Lizzie replied, her voice turning slightly shrill with desperation, 'is getting you out of my bedroom and my house. You may be my boss, but you don't have any rights in here.'

'I wouldn't want any,' he scoffed, and too late Lizzie realised how it had sounded. Bedroom rights. Sexual rights. With a small smile, he bent down and hooked the strap of her discarded bra on his little finger, dangling it in front of her. 'A bit too small for my taste.'

She flushed, thought of threatening a sexual harassment suit and knew she never would. 'Please leave,' she said in a voice that was entirely too weak and wavery, and realised with a stab of mortification that there were actually tears in her eyes. She was pathetic. Cormac certainly thought so.

'Gladly,' he informed her, 'but you're coming with me.'

Lizzie blinked. The threat of tears had thankfully receded, leaving only bafflement. 'Coming with you? Why?'

'You don't have the proper clothes,' Cormac said as if speaking to an idiot, 'so we'll have to get you some.'

'I don't want—'

'This isn't about what you want, Miss Chandler. It's about what *I* want. Get that straight right now.'

Lizzie bit hard on her lip. She couldn't afford to dig in her heels now, not over something like this. She needed her job, her salary, especially now Dani was at university, requiring fees, living costs, books and a bit to enjoy herself with. Lizzie couldn't afford to antagonise Cormac Douglas, especially not over a few outfits.

'Fine,' she finally said, her voice clipped. 'I assume you're footing the bill?'

He smiled. It made her insides curl unpleasantly. 'Of course. You couldn't afford a pair of panties from the place we're going.'

'I wouldn't want any,' Lizzie snapped, but he'd already walked out of the bedroom, no doubt expecting her to follow, trotting at his heels.

CHAPTER TWO

LIZZIE sat stiffly on a cream leather sofa while Cormac spoke in a hushed voice to the sales assistant at the expensive boutique he'd brought her to on Princes Street.

What kind of man inspired the respect, awe and, most likely, fear that kept an exclusive boutique open for its only customer at eight o'clock at night?

The answer was right in front of her, in the arrogant, authoritative stance and the assessingly dismissive look Cormac shot her before turning back to the assistant.

'Don't let her choose her own clothes. She wouldn't know what to pick.'

Lizzie pressed her lips together and gazed blindly out of the rain-smeared window. He was right; she wouldn't know what to pick. But he didn't have to tell the assistant that, and certainly not in that tone.

On the taxi ride to the boutique, she'd made the decision not to get angry at Cormac's rude and arrogant ways. She just wouldn't care.

He was *known* as ruthless and cold, she reminded herself; he was indifferent to the point of rudeness. He was also respected because of his incredible talent and building designs.

Right now those designs didn't seem to matter very much.

'All right, miss.' The assistant, a sleek woman in a grey silk suit, came forward, smiling briskly. 'Mr Douglas would like you to be outfitted for the weekend. Will you come this way?'

With a jerky nod, refusing to look at Cormac, Lizzie followed the assistant into the inner room of the boutique.

'I'm Claire,' the woman called over her shoulder as she began pulling clothes from the racks. 'You'll need at least two evening dresses, some casual wear, a swimming costume…' The list went on, washing over Lizzie in an incomprehensible tide of sound.

She'd never spent much time or money on clothes, never had the inclination or interest, not to mention the means. Now she reached out and stroked a cocktail dress of crimson silk, the material sliding through her fingers like water.

Why was Cormac doing this? Surely, *surely* as his secretary she didn't need clothes like this, no matter how promising or prominent this commission could be.

Did he feel sorry for her? Impossible. Embarrassed for her? *By* her? Lizzie considered it, but decided Cormac Douglas didn't have enough sensitivity towards anyone to feel such an emotion.

So why? Because she knew, more than anything, that Cormac didn't do anything unless there was something in it for him.

'Miss Chandler?' Claire indicated the sumptuous changing room and, with a little apologetic smile, Lizzie entered.

An hour later she was trying on the last outfit, a slinky silver evening dress with skinny straps that poured over her slight curves like liquid moonlight.

Lizzie smoothed the elegant material over her hips, amazed at the transformation. Her pale blond hair fell to her shoulders in a soft cloud, and her eyes were wide and luminous. It looked, she thought ruefully, as if the dress were too big for her, even though it fitted perfectly. She looked overawed by the glamour, and she was.

Just what was Cormac trying to turn her into? Because it wasn't working.

What kind of woman did he want her to be this weekend…and why?

Perhaps she was paranoid to be so suspicious, yet she couldn't shake the unreality of the situation…the impossibility.

'Gorgeous,' Claire murmured, and gestured her to leave the dressing room. 'Mr Douglas will want to see this.'

'I don't think—' Lizzie began, but Claire was already pulling her hand, and from the corner of her eye she saw Cormac stand up, alert and ready, lips pressed together in a firm, hard line.

She stood in the middle of the room, conscious of the way the dress clung to her body and swirled about her feet, leaving very little to the imagination…to Cormac's imagination.

He surveyed her from top to toe, his hazel eyes darkening, his face expressionless.

'Good,' he said after a moment. 'Add it to the rest.'

With a nod, he dismissed her. Feeling like a show pony, Lizzie retreated to the dressing room and peeled off the evening gown, adding it to the heap of clothes that had to cost at least several thousand pounds piled next to her.

'I'll just take these to the front,' Claire said, and Lizzie felt she had to protest.

'I don't really need…' she began, and Claire shook her head.

'Mr Douglas said you might protest, but he was very firm, Miss Chandler. He wants you to be properly outfitted.'

'Does he?' Lizzie muttered, yanking her jeans back on. 'And what Mr Douglas *wants*, Mr Douglas *gets*.'

'That's right.'

With a little yelp Lizzie whirled around and saw Cormac standing in the doorway of the dressing room.

'What are you doing here?' she cried.

'Telling you to hurry up.' He braced one hand against the wall, his glinting eyes sweeping over her, his mouth curving in a knowing smile that brought colour rushing to Lizzie's face.

And not just to her face… Lizzie felt her body react to that assessing gaze, felt her breasts, clad only in a greying, worn bra, tighten and swell. She'd never been looked at in this way by a man—any man—and certainly not by a man like Cormac.

She didn't like it. Her body might react, treacherous and helpless, but her mind and heart rebelled against the assessing way his eyes raked over her, a mocking little smile playing about his mouth.

She put her hands on her hips and lifted her chin. 'Had a good look?'

She thought she saw a flicker of surprise in Cormac's eyes

before he smiled coolly. 'Not much to see.' He turned away before she could reply, and Lizzie put on her shirt with shaking fingers.

Outside the boutique, a pile of boxes and bags at their feet, Cormac hailed a taxi.

Rain still misted down, as soft as a caress, but cold on Lizzie's face. 'I'll see you tomorrow,' he said as the driver loaded her parcels into the car. 'Make sure you bring all of that. I want you dressed properly.'

'So you've said.' Lizzie realised she should probably say thank-you, as he'd spent a rather indecent amount of money on her, but somehow she couldn't get herself to form the words. She hadn't wanted the clothes, and he was too overbearing and obnoxious for her to feel any proper gratitude.

The boxes were loaded, the driver waiting, and still, Cormac paused. 'That silver evening dress,' he finally said, his voice gruff. 'Wear that the last night.'

Lizzie opened her mouth to reply, her mind blank. Nothing came out.

'See you at the airport.' Without waiting for a response, he turned away and began walking down the street.

Lizzie watched him go, saw the rain dampen his coat and his hair, and wondered yet again just what kind of man he was…and what she was letting herself in for this weekend.

Lizzie was breathless and flushed when she finally checked in and made her way to the first-class lounge at the airport.

Cormac, the lady at the register had informed her, had checked in half an hour earlier.

Lizzie gritted her teeth. If she hadn't had all those ridiculous bags, filled with clothes she couldn't possibly need, she might have made better time.

'You're late.' Cormac looked up from his sheaf of papers, frowning, as Lizzie made her way into the lounge.

'I'm sorry,' she said stiffly. 'I'm not used to travelling with so much luggage.'

Cormac turned back to his papers. 'I doubt you're used to travelling at all,' he replied, and Lizzie opened her mouth to retort something stinging, but closed it without even framing a response.

What could she say? It was true, and she could hardly argue with her boss anyway. Still, she wished he wasn't right. She wished he didn't know it.

She sank into the seat across from him, conscious of the outfit she wore—slim-fitting black trousers and a cranberry silk blouse, unbuttoned at the throat. She'd pulled her hair back with a clip and fine wisps fell about her flushed face. So much for looking smart.

Cormac lifted his eyes, let his gaze travel slowly over her, from her tousled hair to the pair of black leather pumps that pinched her feet. Lizzie tried not to squirm.

'You should have had your hair cut,' he remarked, and then turned back to his work.

Stung, Lizzie replied, 'If you wanted me to have a complete makeover, you should have given me a bit more warning. As it is, I have no idea why the Hassells will be analysing your secretary!'

He continued to scan the papers as he replied, 'I think I've already explained to you what kind of impression I—*we*—need to make.'

'And you're afraid a bad hair day is going to make or break the deal?' Lizzie jibed, only to fall silent at Cormac's icy look.

'Nothing will break this deal,' he said in a tone that was ominous in its finality. 'Nothing.'

'Perhaps you could tell me a little bit more about what to expect, then,' Lizzie said after a moment. The freezing look in Cormac's eyes thawed only slightly and she tried for a conversational tone. 'Will there be other guests?'

'Later,' he replied, and she knew she was dismissed.

Sinking back into her seat, she gazed around the lounge, the deep leather armchairs seating a variety of well-heeled travellers. Even in her shiny new outfit, Lizzie felt like an outsider. A misfit. She'd never even been on an aeroplane before.

She turned her attention back to Cormac, sneaked a peep at him from beneath her lashes. He was deeply absorbed in his work, his eyes downcast, his own lashes, thick and dark, sweeping and softening the harsh planes of his face.

He was a harsh man, Lizzie thought, and felt, for the first time, a rush of curiosity about what—or who—had made him the way he was.

Ruthless, ambitious, unfeeling. Cold. The tabloids had used every damning word, delighting in Cormac's reviled reputation. The women—starlets and socialites alike—flocked to him, to the bad boy they mistakenly thought they could tame.

Now Lizzie wondered why. *Why are you the way you are?*

Everyone had a past, a story. She thought of her own—her parents' death ten years ago, Dani's dependence. The life she'd made for herself, caring for Dani, providing her younger sister with every opportunity and affection.

She'd rung Dani to explain about the weekend, only to have her sister blithely assure her that Lizzie could do whatever she wanted, Dani was already busy with her own life.

Lizzie knew it was ridiculous to feel hurt. Rejected. Yet she did. She was glad Dani was so happy at university. She was *thrilled*.

She knew she was.

It just didn't feel that way right now.

Cormac looked up. 'They're boarding first class.'

He stood up, putting his papers back in his attaché case. Lizzie saw a glimpse of sketches, strong pencil lines that didn't look like the usual architectural blueprints, but they were slipped out of sight before she could guess what they were.

Clutching her handbag, she followed Cormac into the queue. They'd already been assigned seats and the airline attendants were cloyingly deferential as they led Cormac to two sumptuous reclining seats in soft grey leather.

Lizzie followed behind, feeling out of place and yet helplessly giddy at the blatant luxury. The feelings intensified when they sat down and an attendant offered them champagne and a crystal bowl full of strawberries.

Lizzie took the flute awkwardly, rotated the fragile crystal stem between her slick fingers. 'Some service.'

'First class,' Cormac dismissed, and pushed his glass away, untouched.

Lizzie took a cautious sip. She hadn't had champagne in years, not since before her parents had died, and then only a sip or two on Hogmanay or birthdays. Now the bubbles tickled her throat and her nose, made her feel a bit dizzy.

Or was it just the total unreality of the situation, sitting in first class, sipping champagne with Cormac Douglas?

Cormac was staring broodingly out of the window, the bare, brown fields and leafless trees stark against a slate-grey sky. Lizzie put her champagne flute down and glanced around at the other first-class passengers settling themselves.

A polished woman in designer denim shot her a look of pure envy and, startled, Lizzie realised the woman must think she and Cormac were a couple.

Lovers.

She glanced back at her boss, still lost in his own thoughts. His face was in profile and she could see the strong, clean line of his jaw. She was close enough even to see the glint of gold stubble on his chin, the way his close-cropped brown hair was streaked by the sun.

She turned away abruptly.

Soon the rest of the passengers were settled and the plane began to taxi towards the runway. Lizzie leaned back in her seat, her nerves beginning a sudden, frantic flutter in her middle.

Cormac saw her fingers curl around the armrest and raised one eyebrow. 'Are you nervous?'

'A bit,' she admitted unwillingly. 'I've never flown before.'

'But you had a passport.'

'I went to Paris by train once.' As an escort for Dani's fifth form field trip, but she let Cormac think what he liked.

Apparently he didn't think much for he raised his eyebrows and murmured, 'I see.'

Soon the plane was lifting into a steely sky and Lizzie felt her stomach dip. Once the craft levelled out, she felt more relaxed and her fingers loosened on the armrest.

Above the clouds, the sky was a deep, clear purple, a cloak of twilight, smooth and soft. Lizzie let out a little sigh.

The attendant came to take drink orders and she asked for an orange juice. Cormac asked for the same.

Once the attendant had moved on, he turned to her, eyes suddenly flinty and cold. His mouth was set and a furrow was in the middle of his forehead. 'We need to talk.'

Lizzie set her orange juice down. 'Okay.'

'Your role in this weekend's meetings is…important.'

Lizzie raised her eyebrows, bemused. Shorthand and shuffling papers was important? 'I understand,' she began carefully, feeling he required some response, 'that you want to put forth an impeccable—'

'Do you know anything about the Hassells?' he demanded, cutting her off, and Lizzie shrugged.

'Only what you've told me. They own an island in the Dutch Antilles, and they finally want to build a resort there.'

His mouth thinned and he reached down to extract a newspaper clipping from his attaché case. 'Read that.'

Lizzie took the clipping with cautious curiosity. *The Hassells: A Family, A Dynasty* the headline read. The article described the family, a Dutch dynasty that had lived on Sint Rimbert for over a hundred years. She read about Jan Hassell, his wife, Hilda, and their three sons, all entrepreneurs in various cities across the globe.

The family was focused on developing the local economy, keeping the island eco-friendly and retaining 'the family values the Hassells have cherished for a century'. The write-up was glowing indeed, and she looked up to see Cormac scowling at her.

'Now do you understand?'

She didn't. 'They seem like a nice family,' she said as she handed back the clipping. Not the type of people to care about whether a secretary wore designer clothes, either, although she bit her tongue to stop herself from voicing that thought aloud.

'Family values,' Cormac said, glancing down at the article. His voice was a sneer.

His face was dark, as if a storm had gathered in his thoughts. Lizzie struggled for something to say to lighten the mood. 'They're clearly not in it just for the money,' she ventured. The article had described the Hassells' decision to build a resort—'a way of sharing the beauty of our island with the world.' A bit saccharine, perhaps, but a pretty sentiment nonetheless.

'Everyone's in it for the money,' Cormac said flatly. He glanced over at her, his expression now alarmingly neutral. 'The Hassells want an architect with family values, as well,' he continued. 'They've invited three architects to this weekend—the short-list—including me. As far as I can tell, they want everyone sitting round playing Happy Families and singing campfire songs.'

Lizzie stared at him, wondering what was coming next. Cormac Douglas was about as far from family values as a man could get.

'They invited you to Sint Rimbert,' she repeated hesitantly, trying to make sense of what he was telling her. 'So whatever they think about family values…'

'They invited me,' Cormac interjected, 'because I told them I was newly married and looking forward to having a family.'

Lizzie's mouth dropped open. 'But…that's not true…'

'It is,' he replied with a faint feral smile, 'for the purposes of this weekend.'

Lizzie blinked. Her stomach dipped, dropped. She wanted to make sense of what Cormac was saying, yet she had the odd feeling that if she put two and two together she'd get about twenty. Cormac was gazing at her steadily, coldly, his expression like a vice on her mind. Her soul.

'So…how…?' She shook her head, licked her lips. Her mouth was dry and she took a sip of orange juice. It felt like acid coating her throat. 'What are you trying to tell me?' she finally asked, and her voice came out in little more than a scratchy whisper.

'I'm telling you,' Cormac replied with icy precision, 'that this weekend you're not my secretary. You're my wife.'

CHAPTER THREE

FOR one tantalising second the word conjured images in Lizzie's mind she had no business thinking of. *Wife*. Entwined fingers, tangled limbs. Marriage, love. Sex.

She blinked. 'Your wife?' she repeated. 'But…how?' She shook her head. 'You mean, pretend?'

His mouth curved into a smile she didn't like and his eyes remained cold. 'Did you think I was asking you for real?'

'You mean, lie?' Lizzie clarified. The realisation of what he was asking her to do rolled through her in sickening waves. 'Deceive the people you want to work for so you can get your blasted commission?'

Cormac looked unruffled. 'I suppose that's not putting too fine a point on it,' he agreed with deceptive mildness.

It was all making sense now—the reason he'd asked her to accompany him so suddenly, the importance of looking the part with cases of designer clothes. Even his request to call him by his first name. All part of a deception. A lie.

Lizzie looked away, closed her eyes.

It was impossible. It was wrong. She couldn't pretend to be Cormac's wife—she didn't like him, didn't even *know* him. Pulling off such a charade would be ludicrous; she wouldn't be able to keep it up for a minute, even if she wanted to…

For a moment Lizzie pictured what such an act would require. Shared looks, jokes, bodies, beds.

A thrill darted through her, tempting, treacherous. She couldn't…wouldn't…*want to*…

She glanced back at him, saw him lounging comfortably in his seat, an expression of arrogant amusement in his eyes as if he'd witnessed her entire thought process.

Perhaps he had.

She licked her lips. 'Even if I agreed—which I'm not—how would it actually work? You're famous, Cormac.' Her mouth twisted. 'Notorious. If Jan Hassell is interested in hiring you, he will have researched your background. All it would take is one search on the Internet to come up with a dozen stories that refute these so-called family values of yours.' The photos in the tabloids waltzed before her eyes—Cormac with his arm around his latest glamorous conquest, usually replaced within twenty-four hours.

Cormac smiled. 'I'm a reformed man.'

She laughed shortly. 'You'd have to be a pretty good actor to pull that off.'

He leaned forward, eyes glittering, his voice a whisper, a promise. 'I am.'

Lizzie leaned back into her seat. He was too close, too dangerous, too *much*. In that moment, she had no doubt Cormac could pull such a feat off—and she couldn't.

Couldn't risk it.

Could she?

'I can't.' She spoke sharply, too sharply, and saw Cormac smile. He knew too much, saw too much. She shook her head. 'It's wrong. It's immoral.'

'You think so?' He stretched his legs out, took a sip of orange juice. 'Actually, you'll find that what the Hassells are doing is wrong. If not immoral, then at least some shade of illegal.'

'What do you mean?'

He raised one eyebrow. 'Discrimination, Chandler. What if I were gay? Or a widower? They'd be discriminating against me by insisting I be married.'

'But you're not gay,' she snapped, and he inclined his head in acknowledgement.

'Of course not, but the principle remains the same, don't you think?'

She shook her head in mute, instinctive denial. She didn't

want things twisted. She didn't want to *think*. 'It's still a deception.'

'Yes. But for a good reason.'

'It doesn't matter—'

'You're right.' Cormac cut her off smoothly. He was still relaxed, smiling even, while she was clutching her chair as if it would keep her grounded. Safe.

Which it wouldn't. The whole world was spinning, reeling.

'What matters,' he continued, 'is the resort. The design. And I'll build a spectacular resort—you know that.' It wasn't a question, and Lizzie didn't bother answering it.

Yes. She knew. Once upon a time, she'd had artistic ambitions of her own. She'd seen Cormac's designs and, while she was no architect, she recognised good work. Brilliant work. 'The Hassells must have some reason for wanting a married architect,' Lizzie insisted. She heard the weakness, the doubt in her own voice. So did Cormac.

'Probably,' he agreed. 'I just don't care what it is.'

'How would you expect to pull it off? You don't even know me…'

'I know enough.'

'Do you even know my first name?' Lizzie asked, cutting him off. A bubble of laughter verging on hysteria rose in her throat; she swallowed it down. 'How on earth do you see yourself acting as my reformed, loving husband when you don't even know my name?' She shook her head, still too stunned to be scared. 'The whole idea is ludicrous!'

Cormac cocked his head, gazed at her for a moment with hard, thoughtful eyes. Then he smiled.

Normally when Cormac smiled, it was a cold, sardonic curving of his mobile mouth.

Now it was something tender, promising, sensual. His eyes flicked over her slim form with heavy-lidded intent, his mouth curved—curved knowingly, lovingly—and something unfurled in Lizzie's middle and spiralled upwards, taking over her heart, her mind.

Her will.

'No…' she whispered, and she didn't even know what she was

protesting against except that look and what it meant. What it promised.

And she didn't even understand what that was.

Cormac leaned forward, brushed his knuckles across her cheek. The simple touch sent that spiralling emotion hurtling through her body—every limb, every bone and muscle—until she sagged against her seat.

'Yes,' he murmured languorously.

Lizzie shook herself, watched as he moved closer, his lips hovering inches from hers. His lashes swept downward, hiding those cruel eyes, and his lips brushed her ear. 'Yes,' he whispered again, and she shivered. Shuddered.

She felt him shift back, realised she'd closed her eyes, let her head fall back.

She was so pathetic. And he knew.

'I think,' he said in a voice laced with cool amusement, 'you'll find I'm a good enough actor. We'll pull it off.'

'You might be good enough,' Lizzie choked, 'but I'm not.'

Cormac paused. Smiled. 'Perhaps,' he said softly, 'you don't need to act.'

Shame and fury scorched her soul, her face. She drew in a desperate breath.

Cormac leaned forward as a flight attendant approached them. 'Could we have some more champagne? We've just been married and we're celebrating.'

Lizzie jerked, saw the flight attendant coo at Cormac. 'Of course, sir.' She glanced briefly at Lizzie, seemed unimpressed and turned away.

Cormac sat back in his seat and smiled. Smirked.

'You shouldn't have said that,' Lizzie said. Her heart was still thudding against her ribs, adrenalin pouring through her, turning her weak. She had been so weak. For a moment—a second—she'd been transfixed by Cormac. *Cormac*. The man who had not had a single kind word, glance or even thought for her.

She was disgusted with herself. 'I haven't agreed to anything yet and I don't plan to. Even if you're perfectly capable of convincing the Hassells that we're married,' she told him, grateful that her voice didn't shake, 'that you're in *love* with me, I won't agree. I won't.' She sounded petulant. A smile flickered over Cormac's face and was gone.

'Yes, you will.' He spoke calmly, conversationally. As if he had no doubt. Sickeningly, Lizzie realised that he probably didn't.

She gave a little laugh of disbelief; it trembled on the air. 'What are you going to do?' she asked. 'Threaten to fire me? Somehow I don't think that would hold up in a court of law.'

'Are you saying you'd sue me?' Cormac murmured, and Lizzie flushed. She didn't know if she had the stamina to suffer through a lawsuit, the time and money it would cost. The publicity, the shame.

'Are you saying,' she countered, her voice shaking enough now for both of them to notice, 'that you'd blackmail me?'

'Here you are, sir.' The flight attendant returned with two flutes of fizzy champagne, smiling sycophantically at Cormac, who returned it with a quick, playful grin that blazed along Lizzie's nerve-endings even though it wasn't directed at her.

She'd never been *affected* by this man before. Hadn't remotely expected it. Didn't like it.

The attendant left and Cormac pushed his drink to the side. He eyed her thoughtfully, as if she were a puzzle to be completed, a problem to be sorted. '*Blackmail* is a dirty word,' he said after a moment. 'Not one I prefer to use.'

'A rose by any other name…' Lizzie quoted, and he chuckled.

'Is it blackmail, Chandler, to buy you clothes? To take you to a luxurious villa in the Caribbean, all expenses paid?' He leaned forward. 'Or would people—the press—consider it a bribe? An accepted bribe.'

She stilled, her eyes widening in dawning realisation. 'You're saying no one would believe me if I told them you were blackmailing me?'

'I think they'd be more likely to believe that you were a spurned lover. Imagine the press, sweetheart. The tremendously bad press.'

'Don't call me sweetheart,' Lizzie snapped, and he shrugged.

She looked away, tried to quell the roiling nausea that his words had caused.

Suddenly she saw it all in a different, dreadful light. Against Cormac's calm confidence, she would be a hopeless, helpless wreck. Even if she managed to stammer a defence, no one would believe her. No one would even want to.

The press would be merciless, relishing the scandal. She would be judged, condemned as some sort of cheap gold-digger. Her career would be ruined.

So would Cormac's.

She turned back to him. 'Even if telling the truth ruined me, it would ruin you, too. Everyone would know you'd asked me to pretend—you've already told the Hassells you're married!' Her eyes narrowed and she gathered the courage to hiss, 'Somehow I think you have a lot more to lose than I do.'

He steepled his fingers under his chin, eyebrows raised. 'Do I?'

'You seem to want this commission rather a lot. Why is that?'

He shrugged, even as Lizzie saw a flicker of something—desolation? determination?—in his eyes before it was gone. 'It's important to me. A challenge.' He gazed at her calmly, his eyes now hard and bright, and yet something in that brief flicker had snagged Lizzie's curiosity. Her sympathy. She knew he wasn't telling the truth—the whole truth.

But what was the truth? She had no way of discovering it, no way of knowing.

'Still,' she pressed, 'you're taking a huge risk just for one commission. Your entire career could go up in flames! Even if I agree, someone else might discover the truth…' She shook her head slowly as she considered the implications. 'And even if this weekend was a success, there would be other times. You'd be working on the design for this resort for a year at least. How would you explain the fact that you're not married any more?'

He shrugged. 'A divorce? A separation? Perhaps I'd simply say you were at home, waiting for me.' He smiled, although there was an intense, icy light in his eyes that made Lizzie want to shiver.

'The press would get wind of it…'

'The Hassells are never in the British press,' Cormac dismissed. 'And I'm the only British architect on this weekend. No-body from England even knows I'm going.'

'But they'll find out when you receive the commission,' Lizzie argued, and Cormac leaned forward.

'Does that mean you're agreeing?' he murmured with sleepy languor.

Lizzie stiffened. 'Do I really have much choice?' It hadn't taken long to realise just how cornered she truly was. Cormac had coldly, calculatingly built the evidence against her. He'd waited until they were on the plane before telling her—there was no escape without shaming them both.

'You could tell Hassell when we land,' Cormac offered. 'I expect he'd believe you. All those family values…' He waved a hand in contemptuous dismissal. 'They must count for something when it comes to a damsel in distress.'

'Yes, and then what? He'll send us both back on the very next plane, and no doubt tell the press what you've done. Your career would be ruined, and so would mine. And you know how rabid tabloid journalists can be. They'd be sniffing around me… around…' She stopped abruptly and looked away.

'Around your sister?' Cormac finished, and Lizzie jerked back to face him.

'What do you know about my sister?'

'You've been taking care of her for ten years or so, since your parents died,' Cormac replied calmly. 'She's what? Eighteen? Impressionable, probably. I imagine that so much publicity could go to her head quite quickly.' He smiled.

Lizzie swallowed, tasted bile. She could just about face her own career—her own *life*—being ruined. But not Dani's. Nothing could happen to Dani.

She hadn't spent the last ten years saving and sacrificing to have Dani's chances at a better life shot to hell…and all because of Cormac.

Cormac. This was all his fault…and there was nothing she could do about it.

'How do you know so much?' she demanded in a furious, frightened whisper, and he shrugged.

'Most of it is on your CV.'

'So is my name!' She felt like scratching that arrogant, indulgent smile right off his mouth.

'Yes,' he agreed, 'but that information isn't important to me.'

'It should be, if you want to pretend to be my husband!' She'd raised her voice and in one quick, quiet movement Cormac grabbed her wrist, encased her hand in his like a vice. He pressed her fingers against her own mouth in a movement that was almost tender, except for the look in his eyes.

His eyes were cold. Freezing, dangerous. Dead.

'Careful, Chandler,' he whispered. 'You don't really want to give the game away now, do you?'

'Yes, I do,' she choked. She wrenched her hand out of his grasp. 'You're such a—'

'Now, now,' he murmured, smiling, although his eyes were still cold, still frighteningly flat. Lizzie choked back her words, her fear.

A flight attendant passed, glancing at them curiously.

She probably thought this was a lovers' spat, Lizzie thought. A little tiff. If it weren't quite so horrible, it would have been funny.

Except Lizzie did not feel like laughing.

'Why?' she asked, and it came out in a wretched whisper. 'Why are you doing this? It's only one commission. And it's such a risk—you could be ruining both of our lives.'

Her head drooped and she pressed the heels of her hands to her eyes, willed the tears and despair back.

Cormac was silent. 'If you make it through this weekend,' he finally told her, his voice soft, 'I'll pay you double your normal salary for the rest of the year. I'll make sure you never receive a word of bad press—even if it all comes out.'

Lizzie looked up bleakly. 'How can you make sure of that?'

'I can. Trust me, Chandler. I don't take foolish risks.'

'This seems pretty foolish to me,' she retorted, and he smiled.

'Yes, and foolhardy…and a little bit interesting, don't you think?' He leaned forward, his lids lowering, his lashes sweeping the bronzed planes of his face. His breath feathered her hair, her cheek. 'A bit intriguing, perhaps…' he murmured, a provocative, questioning lilt to his voice.

Lizzie stared at him, amazed by his sudden transformation. Transfixed by it. 'No,' she denied—a matter of instinct. Protection. *No.*

'It could be an adventure,' Cormac continued, his voice turning silkily persuasive. 'For both of us.' His eyes glittered and again she saw that flicker, as if something had been stripped away or dropped into place. She didn't know which.

What was it? It was a shadow, a veil, and yet it also revealed. Revealed the man beneath the hard veneer of calculated charm—if there was one.

'An adventure? I don't...' Lizzie's breath hitched as she dragged it into her lungs '...see how.'

Cormac raised his eyebrows, a smile played about his mouth. His lips were both sculpted and soft...and close. Very close. To her.

'Don't you?' he murmured. He raised one hand to her cheek and twined her hair through his fingers. With each sleepy spiral of his hand he ticked off a point. 'You'll be in the Caribbean, in a beautiful villa. Wined and dined with a trunkful of designer clothes at your disposal—clothes which cost a small fortune. Petted, pampered. What woman wouldn't enjoy that?'

Lizzie swallowed. What woman, indeed? She wanted to say *she* wouldn't, insist that she couldn't be bought so easily, and yet...

There was truth in his words.

Some bizarre, yearning part of her wanted this. Not the clothes, perhaps, or the food or any of the luxuries Cormac thought would entice her.

She wanted the thrill. The adventure, the intimacy. She'd had precious little in her life so far. The last ten years had been a desert of devotion to her sister.

She wanted excitement...and she wanted it with Cormac.

Cormac—the boss she barely knew, who had no interest in knowing her. Yet who was now looking at her, his eyes glittering, a smile of tempting, sensuous promise stealing over his features, softening them...

Stop. *Stop.*

This was Cormac. This was wrong.

'What about you?' she whispered, hating the need and weakness in her voice. 'How would it be an adventure for you?'

His smile deepened and he dipped closer so his lips touched her ear, sent delicious shivers straight to her soul.

'Why,' he whispered, 'because I'd be with you.' His lips hovered by her ear, making the little hairs on the nape of her neck quiver with awareness. Awareness of him, awareness of need. Need of him. She'd never needed anyone. Not like this. Never like this.

How had she not missed it? How had she *managed* without?

The adrenalin, the adventure, they were an addiction. She felt alive, more alive than she'd ever felt before, every nerve and sense twanging with delicious awareness.

And yet it was wrong...

Wonderfully wrong.

'So?' Cormac breathed, his lips still close to her ear. 'What's your answer...Lizzie?'

He'd known her name. The whole time, she realised, he'd known her name. And somehow, stupidly, that made a difference. That made it almost safe.

She closed her eyes, took in a breath, felt it fill her lungs, felt herself go dizzy. Dizzy, scared and wonderfully excited.

Nothing like this had ever happened to her...and nothing ever would again.

Seize life.

Seize it.

'Yes,' she whispered. 'I'll do it.'

She felt Cormac's smile, his lips touched her neck in the barest of kisses. 'I can't wait,' he murmured, and sat back in his seat.

She couldn't even look at him. Cormac smiled to himself, shaking his head slightly at her ridiculous naïveté, her unbelievable innocence. She was embarrassed by the barest brush of a kiss... He wondered if she were a virgin.

She was twenty-eight years old. Surely not. That, he mused, would really be just too pathetic.

Yet it could also prove to be interesting...

Ever since seeing her in that silver gown—and then afterwards in her worn-out bra and jeans—he'd considered whether he would sleep with her. Seduce her. It would be easy, really, all too revoltingly simple, as his brief taste on the plane journey had already proved. A few whispered words, a little caress, and she'd fallen into his hands like softened clay, ready to be shaped to his own desire. His own purpose. He usually liked a bit more of a challenge.

Still…seduction had its uses. A Lizzie who believed herself in love might be more pliable than one who was simply going along because she'd been coerced.

On the other hand, a Lizzie who felt she'd been ruthlessly seduced could be dangerous. Unpredictable.

He'd have to be cautious. Lizzie Chandler needed careful handling.

He gazed out of the window, the stretch of inky sky merely a canvas for the resort he was going to design. The commission he would seize.

The people he would prove wrong.

Lizzie had asked him why this particular commission was so important to him; Cormac hadn't realised just how much it mattered until the question had been voiced aloud.

No one would tell him what he could or couldn't do. No one would tell him he wasn't good enough, worthy enough for anything.

Not any more.

He was in charge, in control of his own destiny—and of hers.

He had Lizzie Chandler in the palm of his hand and that was exactly where he wanted her.

CHAPTER FOUR

AS SOON as their dinners had been cleared—beef fillet and truffle-studded potatoes—Cormac turned brisk and business-like.

After the few terrifying moments when he'd been so soft, so seductive, Lizzie was grateful for the change.

Brisk she could handle. Businesslike she could do.

'So…' Cormac turned to her. The flight attendant had left them with a pot of coffee, two delicate cups and a plate of petit fours. Cormac pushed the sweets aside and took a sip of strong black coffee. He hadn't touched any alcohol during dinner, Lizzie had noticed, and he'd eaten lightly, despite the many rich offerings.

He was, she realised, a man of incredible restraint. Control. Which made what had happened before—the teasing, tempting breath of a kiss—all the more worrisome. He was just flirting with her, teasing her as a form of amusement. Intimidation. He'd obviously seen how affected she was, just as she'd realised how affected he wasn't.

'We need to get our stories straight,' he said now. He took a sip of coffee before reaching for some papers from his attaché case. 'If you're telling Hassell we met at a wine bar and I say we met at work…' he glanced up briefly, eyes lighting with rare humour '…even the most trusting of saints would start to wonder.'

Lizzie nodded. She stirred a spoonful of sugar into her coffee and thought of the silly films she'd seen where just that scenario had occurred. Then had it been funny; now it was frightening.

No matter how exciting it might be, they both still had so much to lose.

'You've thought of a story?' she asked, nodding at the papers.

'Best to keep to the truth as much as possible. Then we're less likely to trip ourselves up. Now, the facts.' He gave her a glimmer of a smile before he began the recitation. 'We've been married six weeks. You've always worked for me, and one day…'

Suddenly Lizzie couldn't help herself. It was a game and she wanted to play. Flirt, even if just for pretend. She wanted to have *fun*. To seize life. 'One day,' she interrupted, smiling with coy promise, 'I walked into your office with some letters for you to sign and you just *realised*.' Cormac glanced at her, eyebrow raised in amused query. Lizzie gave a breathy, delighted sigh. 'You looked into my eyes…' she leaned forward and fluttered her lashes '…and realised that your life had been so cold, so empty, so *meaningless* without me. Didn't you?'

She dared to trail her fingers along his cheek, revelling in the rough stubble, the tick in his jaw. 'It was so sudden, of course. I never thought my boss would be interested in me for one second… But you insisted on taking me out to dinner, and the rest…' she shrugged, gave a little laugh '…is history. Isn't it, darling?' She sat back, smiling triumphantly even though her heart was beating a bit too hard.

She'd meant to take her hand away from his cheek, but he was too fast. He grabbed it, held it to his lips as his eyes roamed, caressed her face. 'That's just how it happened, sweetheart. I'll never forget the moment I realised how hopelessly I'd fallen in love with you.' He kissed the tip of her finger, nibbled on the sensitive pad. Lizzie gasped. Aloud. He smiled and continued nibbling. 'And you,' he murmured in a lower, more seductive voice like the slide of silk on skin, 'fell rather hopelessly in love with me.' He was sucking her fingers, his tongue flicking along her skin, her nerve-endings, his teeth tenderly biting into her flesh, filling her with craven need. Desire. His mouth curved into a smile that was all too knowing, and amusement lit his eyes.

She'd been playing a game and she had the feeling she'd just lost.

With one last brush against his lips, he dropped her hand into her lap. 'Don't lay it on too thick, Chandler, or they'll really start to wonder.' He turned back to his papers, completely unruffled, while Lizzie sagged against the seat.

Lord help her. What the *hell* had she got herself into?

Somehow she managed to get through the next half hour as Cormac droned on about the basics of what they needed to know. She felt frozen, numb. Afraid.

She wasn't sure she could do this after all. At that moment she was more afraid of Cormac than the press. More fearful for her body—her heart—than her career or reputation.

She'd had no idea she would react this way to Cormac, to his touch, his look; she was leaning into it, craving it. Craving *him*. Adventure was one thing; abandon was quite another. Her mind danced with possibilities she had no business entertaining.

This was a charade, she told herself fiercely, not the real thing. Never the real thing.

Help.

Cormac irritably tapped his pen against the sheaf of papers. 'You haven't been listening to a word, have you?'

'Sorry.' She flinched guiltily. 'It's just so much to take in.'

He capped the pen and gestured to the flight attendant to take their empty coffee cups. 'I don't suppose it really matters,' he said with a shrug. 'No one will be expecting a deceit, so no one will be looking for one.'

'No one will think it strange that you've only been married for six weeks?'

'Coincidence rather than convenience,' he replied with a shrug. 'People will expect a newly-wed couple, newly in love, and I don't think it will take much to convince them that's what they're seeing.' He paused, his gaze dipping down to her fingers—the fingers he'd touched. Tasted. 'I'm rather confident of your *acting* abilities.'

Lizzie tried for a laugh; it came out like a wheeze. 'At least it's only for a few days.'

'A few memorable days,' Cormac agreed. His smile turned

languourous, his gaze heavy-lidded. All intentional, Lizzie knew, and yet she wasn't immune. She felt her stomach clench, prepare for an assault of the senses, the flood of damning desire. Cormac's smile deepened. 'Who knows what might happen?'

The cabin lights flickered and dimmed. Cormac leaned over, his arm brushing her breasts—intentional again, Lizzie was sure—and he eased her chair into a reclining position.

Prone, supine before him, Lizzie clutched the armrests. Hated feeling vulnerable.

'Sweet dreams, Chandler,' he whispered. Lizzie lay there and watched as he adjusted his own seat, settled a pillow under his head and promptly fell asleep.

If only it were so easy for her. She lay in the dark, her eyes wide-open, her body thrumming with fear, excitement and un-fulfilled desire.

It was a heady mix.

'We'll be arriving in Bonaire in just under forty minutes.'

Lizzie tilted her seat forward, her eyes gritty from lack of sleep, although she'd finally fallen into a restless doze only to be jerked awake by the bright Caribbean sunlight streaming through the window and the chirpy voice of the flight attendant as she pushed the breakfast cart down the aisle.

Her damp hands curled around the metal buckle of her seat belt. Next to her, Cormac sat relaxed, calm, smiling.

Her husband.

She smiled, a small stretching of her lips. In little over half an hour they would exit in Bonaire, take a small chartered plane to Sint Rimbert and the charade would begin.

She would be Cormac's wife. A thrill of terror rippled through her in an icy wave.

She couldn't eat any of the breakfast, although Cormac was calmly drinking a cup of strong black coffee. Once the dishes had been cleared away, they prepared for landing.

'Here.' Cormac pressed something cool and hard into her palm; Lizzie looked down and saw it was a wedding ring. Platinum. Expensive.

'I can't…' she began, shaking her head. Cormac curled her fingers around the ring.

'Yes,' he said, 'you can.'

Lizzie slipped the ring on with numb fingers. It was a little too big, although not enough for anyone to notice.

She was the only one who would notice, who would care. Who would realise how wrong it felt.

It was too late for regrets, she knew. Far too late for second thoughts. She'd agreed, she'd let Cormac seduce her with his words, his touch, his promise.

Who knows what might happen?

Nothing, Lizzie told herself fiercely now. Absolutely nothing.

It was too dangerous. Too tempting.

The plane landed with a bump.

Cormac stood up, slinging his attaché case over his shoulder. He handed Lizzie her handbag and she started in surprise.

'Here you are, sweetheart,' he said, and she stiffened. He smiled over her head at the flight attendant who'd been ogling him for the entire journey. 'She's always forgetting her things on aeroplanes.'

The attendant tittered, and Lizzie's cheeks burned. 'Ridiculing me to the staff before we've even stepped off the plane?' she hissed. 'What a loving husband you are…darling.'

'Just teasing,' he murmured, but she saw a new flintiness in his eyes and realised she'd scored a direct hit. Pretending to be a loving husband—a loving anything—was going to be difficult for Cormac.

Perhaps as difficult as it was proving to be for her.

A young pilot, smiling and speaking with a Dutch accent, met them as they stepped off the plane. The next half hour was a blur of customs, the glare of the hot sun reflecting off the tin roofs of the airport and giving Lizzie a headache. She barely had time to take in their surroundings before they were on a tiny plane, Cormac relaxed next to her, Lizzie's hand clutching the rail.

It felt as if they were flying a kite.

The pilot grinned at her. 'It's small, but it's perfectly safe.'

Right. She thought of all the accidents she'd read about in the papers that had occurred with planes like these.

This wasn't part of the deal.

What deal? Lizzie asked herself. There was no deal. Cormac

might have let her pretend there was a deal, asked her permission, but it was a joke. A farce.

There was simply Cormac's will and her submission to it.

Why had she not realised that before? Had she actually believed she'd had some *choice*?

She closed her eyes. Cormac patted her hand, a caress that felt like a warning.

'She's just a bit nervous…and tired.' She opened her eyes to see him wink at the pilot, who grinned. Lizzie gritted her teeth.

'There's Sint Rimbert now.' The pilot pointed out of the window and Lizzie craned her neck to see.

Below them, the sea sparkled like a jewel and nestled in its aquamarine folds was a pristine island, magnificent and unspoiled.

For a moment Lizzie forgot the man next to her, and the role he was requiring her to play, and sucked in an awed breath.

A densely forested mountain rose majestically in the centre of the tiny island, framed by a curve of smooth, white sand, the clear azure sea stretching to an endless horizon.

A few buildings nestled against the mountain—cottages in pastel colours with shutters open to the tropical breeze.

'It's beautiful,' she murmured.

'Sint Rimbert is the jewel of the Caribbean,' the pilot stated. 'Untouched by crass tourism…and it will remain that way.' There was a warning in his voice and Cormac smiled easily.

'Absolutely. And the Hassells are more than generous to even consider sharing this piece of paradise with anyone.'

The pilot nodded in agreement and said no more as he began his descent to the island.

The landing strip was a bare brown line of dirt, barely noticeable in its stunning surroundings.

As they stepped off the plane, the air enfolded her in a balmy caress, heavy with the sweet scent of frangipani. The sky above them was a soft, hazy blue, fleecy clouds scudding across its surface.

Lizzie breathed in the warm tropical air, felt it fill her lungs with a fizz of excitement and hope. As long as she could keep her cool—with Cormac as much as with everyone else—she'd be okay.

She could even enjoy this. Maybe.

She wanted to. She wanted to have a weekend to remember.

She might never get the chance again.

A man—short, balding and in his sixties—strode forward. 'Mr Douglas! We are so pleased! So pleased!' He stuck out his hand for Cormac to shake and Lizzie's heart constricted. This had to be Jan Hassell, the man they were deceiving.

Stop it, she commanded herself. She was in too deep now; it was too late to feel guilty.

Hassell turned to her, beaming as he pumped her hand. 'And this must be your wife…' He paused, forehead wrinkling, and Cormac interjected smoothly.

'Elizabeth. But I call her Lizzie.' He spoke the name as if it were an endearment, smiling at her, his gaze a teasing caress.

Refusing to be baited or belittled, Lizzie smiled back, laced her slick fingers with Cormac's. 'Please call me Lizzie, as well,' she murmured, shooting Cormac a coy smile. 'Everyone does, although Cormac likes to think it's his pet name for me.'

Jan clapped his hand in delight. 'But you are so in love! You will have to tell me all about it. My wife, Hilda, will want to know how it all came about.'

More people to deceive. Lizzie hushed the whisper of her conscience. 'Oh, that's girl talk,' she said with a little laugh. 'Hilda and I will have to chat… I'll tell her all of Cormac's secrets.' She smiled and Jan beamed. 'I'm sure you two have a story, as well!'

'Oh, we do,' Jan assured her with a wink. 'Now, you must be tired. Your things have been brought to my car… Come, follow me.'

He turned and headed towards a four-by-four parked near some scrub.

Cormac put his arm around her shoulders—heavy, warm, a warning. 'Come on, sweetheart,' he said easily, but his hand squeezed her shoulder. He murmured in a low voice, 'Don't lay it on with a trowel, Chandler. It's a bit nauseating.'

'I can believe that,' she replied in an angry undertone. 'Acting like you're in love has to be completely foreign to you! Do you love anything but your precious designs?' Smiling again, she laid her head against his shoulder, felt the tension in his muscles, in her own.

Every petty victory cost her something, as well.

Their luggage stowed in the back, Jan opened the rear door for them to enter.

Lizzie clambered in, hoping that Cormac would sit in the front with Jan.

He did not. He climbed in next to her, his large, muscular thigh pressed against hers, his arm around her shoulders once more, drawing her tightly to his side. She could smell his scent—the tang of soap and cedar and something indefinitely masculine, as well.

Jan beamed at them approvingly before taking the driver's seat. As the Jeep left the airstrip, he told them a bit about the island.

'As you know, Cormac, from our discussion, Sint Rimbert is a small island. There is only one village and a population of less than six hundred. We have a flying doctor, two shops and a post office. That is all.' Jan spoke proudly and Lizzie guessed he was glad he'd held out against tawdry tourism for so long.

'Taking the decision to build a resort was difficult,' he continued as he drove the Jeep along a tarmac road, the thick foliage so close to the car that Lizzie could have reached out and grasped a fern or palm. She saw coconut and banana trees and even the curious, wizened face of a green monkey perched among the branches.

'It is very important to us that the resort won't disturb the local population,' Jan said, 'or the environment any more than necessary. This is not simply a money-making operation for us.'

'Of course not,' Cormac agreed. 'And I am grateful that you have preserved this paradise for us. It would be my pleasure— as well as my duty—to continue to preserve it for those fortunate enough to visit.' His voice was smooth and assured without being sycophantic.

He knew how to deal with someone like Jan, Lizzie thought with a tinge of reluctant admiration. How to manipulate him— just as he was manipulating her.

The thought was unwelcome for it held the bitter gall of truth. Her emotions and senses might be quivering with awakened awareness, but Cormac Douglas felt nothing for her. She was a prop, simply to be used. *Only* to be used.

And she'd better not forget it.

Jan turned the Jeep into a private drive, large wooden gates open to the road.

Lizzie's eyes widened at the luxurious surroundings. The road wound through the thick tropical forest before it gave way to landscaped gardens bursting with colour and scent.

Jan drove the Jeep over a little wooden bridge, a still, glassy pond covered in lily pads below.

The road curved close to the sea before revealing a large circular drive and a low rambling villa that seemed to stretch endlessly into the distance, a maze of white stucco and terracotta roof tiles.

'*Onze Parel*,' he said fondly as he stopped the Jeep and gazed fondly at his home. 'Our Pearl. My great-grandfather named it, and truly it has been a pearl beyond price.'

'Your family has been on this island for a hundred years?' Lizzie queried, feeling both curious and a need to say something.

'Yes. It was sparsely populated before that, mostly with convicts and pirates. Then my great-grandfather received part of the island from Queen Wilhelmina of the Netherlands, as payment for services in the Boer War. He improved the harbour so that ships could land safely—part of the reason Sint Rimbert has been so scarcely populated—and built a plantation.' He smiled sadly. 'It was a sugar plantation, built inland, but the house burned down in the nineteen seventies and the plantation dwindled. We built this villa soon after.'

Lizzie nodded. She was fascinated by the history, yet she also wondered if the building of the resort had more financial motivation than Jan Hassell had let on.

'Come,' he said, 'and Hilda will show you to your rooms. You will want to rest before dinner.'

Cormac climbed out of the Jeep, holding his hand out for Lizzie to grasp as she stepped down. She took it as a matter of course and wasn't prepared for the jolt of sensation that shot up her arm and down to her toes when Cormac's cool, dry fingers encased her own.

He glanced at her, eyes dark, sardonic. Knowing.

He knew too damn much.

She dropped his hand and strode towards the villa.

Wide wooden doors opened to a tiled foyer and lounge, decorated more for comfort and practicality than to impress. Still, it impressed Lizzie. The windows were open, the wooden shutters thrown wide to an open-air corridor that led to the bedrooms. Only metres away Lizzie could see a strip of white sand and the jewel-toned sea.

'Welcome, welcome.' Jan's wife, Hilda, entered the room. Like Jan, she was short and plump, her white hair elegantly coiffed. She wore loose, flowing trousers and a white silk blouse and she looked cool and comfortable and happy for them to be in her home.

Lizzie's sense of discomfort and guilt at deceiving these people returned with a sharp pang. As if he knew, Cormac reached out and clasped her hand, twining her fingers with his as she had done earlier. It was an intimate, proprietary gesture and Hilda saw it and smiled.

As Cormac had known she would.

'You must be tired,' she said, still smiling. 'Let me show you your room.'

Room. Not rooms. And no doubt with one bed. Of course they would be sharing a room; they would most likely be sharing a bed. Lizzie had been dimly aware of this earlier, but now it came to her with nauseating force as Hilda led them down the corridor, hibiscus and orchids spilling from pots, their sweet fragrance heavy on the air, making Lizzie's stomach roil all the more.

Hilda opened a mahogany door and Lizzie took in the room— a wide wooden bed with linen sheets the centrepiece. The tiled floor was scattered with colourful woven rugs and the windows had only shutters, like the rest of the house, now thrown open to the sea.

'I hope you will be comfortable,' Hilda murmured. 'Your bags will be here shortly. Dinner is at eight; we like to gather in the lounge at seven. But please, rest. Enjoy.' She left them quietly, amidst their murmured thanks, and the door closed with a soft click.

'Not bad.' Cormac strode to the window, loosening his tie. Lizzie sank on to the bed. She felt exhausted, strung out. She trembled with tension.

'I can't do this.'

'You just did.'

'I'll never be able to keep it up all weekend,' she protested vainly, for Cormac simply raised his eyebrows.

'You don't really have any choice,' he stated coolly, 'do you?'

He'd loosened his tie and now he tossed it on to a chair. 'Just enjoy yourself,' he continued. 'I plan to.' His fingers went to his shirt, but Lizzie's mind was buzzing too much to notice.

Had he meant that he would enjoy himself or enjoy *her*? Somehow she had the feeling he wanted her to wonder.

'There must be a hundred women in Edinburgh who you could have asked to do this,' she said. 'They would have been glad to. Why me?'

He paused, eyeing her thoughtfully. 'I thought it would be simpler.'

'Simpler!' Lizzie gave a bark of laughter. *Nothing* about this weekend felt simple. 'How?'

'Because we haven't slept together,' Cormac explained with a little smile. 'Yet.'

Lizzie was left staring, gaping at him, the breath robbed from her lungs, her brain...

'Close your mouth, Chandler,' Cormac said, laughter lacing his voice. 'There are flies in the Caribbean. Big ones.'

'We're not...'

'No,' he agreed, the laughter replaced with a thoughtful smile, 'we're not.'

Yet. Did Cormac actually want to sleep with her? Have an affair... Flirting was one thing, but this...

This was dangerous. This was scary.

Lizzie knew she was innocent—more innocent than Cormac even realised. What she didn't know was how to handle this situation. How to handle Cormac. She laughed tonelessly. Cormac wasn't the kind of man to be handled.

If anyone was going to be handled, it was her. She was so out of her depth, she was drowning.

And Cormac was the only one who could save her.

He watched her now, smiling faintly, and Lizzie hated the way he seemed to know what she was thinking, as if her thoughts and fears—not to mention her desires—flashed across her face in neon lights.

Maybe they did.

She rose from the bed, unzipped her suitcase and began to hang up the clothes Cormac had bought her. She needed to be busy. She needed to stop thinking so much. Imagining so much. Cormac. Her and Cormac.

Stop.

'You can always do that later,' Cormac said mildly, and Lizzie shook her head.

'The clothes will get wrinkled.'

'There are servants here, you know.' His voice was lazy, low and rumbling. Lizzie shook her head again; she felt like a marionette.

'I don't want to make a fuss.'

'No,' he murmured, 'you never do.'

A flash of agonised awareness jolted her, made her realise afresh just how expertly Cormac had judged her. Played her.

'Do you use everybody?' she asked, trying to keep her voice conversational. 'Or just me?'

Cormac was silent for a moment; she concentrated on the clothes. 'Everybody,' he said after a moment. 'So don't take it personally.'

She gritted her teeth, guarded herself against the little stab of hurt. 'Oh, I won't.'

Cormac strode towards her, plucked the garment she'd balled uselessly in her hand. 'Talk about wrinkles.' He smoothed it out; it was a filmy silk negligee.

Lizzie snatched it back. 'I'm not wearing that,' she warned him. 'I only brought it because you told me to.'

'Good girl.' His smile was so mocking it made her want to scream. To slap his face.

Then she noticed he had no shirt on. His chest was smooth

and brown, taut with muscle. Just a glimpse of the flat plane of his stomach had Lizzie swallowing and gulping and desperate for air.

'Where is your shirt?' she demanded shrilly.

'On the floor.' He raised one eyebrow. 'We've been flying all night and I'm tired. I'm going to sleep. You should, too.'

She shook her head. 'Cormac, don't...don't try to intimidate me.'

'I thought I was trying to undress.'

They amounted to the same thing, but she wasn't going to say it. He knew, anyway. Somehow she found the strength to drag her gaze to his face which, even though it was sardonic and knowing, was safer. 'We need to lay some ground rules.'

'Such as?'

'You wear clothes in my presence,' Lizzie snapped, 'for starters.'

'Wouldn't it be easier,' Cormac countered, 'to just get used to each other's bodies? People are bound to notice if we blush and stammer every time we catch a little glimpse of skin.'

Lizzie knew only one of them would be blushing or stammering. She ran her hands through her hair and let out a frustrated sigh that half turned into a yelp. 'I wish I'd never agreed to this!'

'But you did,' Cormac replied, unruffled, taking off his belt, 'and now you're just getting cold feet.' He tossed the belt onto a chair and began to unbutton his trousers.

Lizzie flung out a hand. *'Don't.'*

'Chandler, you're being ridiculous.' He sounded annoyed. 'Stop being a prude and get undressed. Didn't you realise it would be like this when you agreed?'

'I thought you'd be a gentleman!'

His voice turned hard. 'Then I suppose you were mistaken.'

Lizzie's eyes were squeezed shut but she heard the whisper of sliding fabric and knew he'd undressed. She heard him move to the bed, and opened one eye to glimpse a broad, muscled back tapering to narrow hips and, fortunately, a pair of boxers.

He was wearing underwear. Thank God.

'You can stand there all afternoon if you'd like,' Cormac informed her, 'but I'm going to sleep.'

It only took Lizzie a few seconds to realise how ridiculous she really was being. Every shocked gasp and prudish look gave Cormac more weapons to use against her. More power.

She took in a shuddering breath, not caring if he heard, and resumed unpacking. Despite her resolve, she wasn't quite ready to get into that bed.

Cormac's breathing was deep and even before she finally decided to change into her own pyjamas—ones she'd brought from home—faded, comfortable and baggy. She glanced at him one last time to make sure he was asleep before she quickly slipped out of her clothes, grateful for the soft, cool cotton against her skin.

Lizzie moved to the bed and lifted the sheet. She glimpsed Cormac's midriff, a whorl of hair leading to the waistband of his boxers, and jerked her glance away.

The sheets were cool and smooth, but Lizzie felt as if she were on fire. She lay there, stiff and straight, painfully, achingly aware of Cormac's relaxed body next to hers.

She shifted on to her side away from him, curled up into a protective little ball.

She heard Cormac stir, felt his breath against her skin. 'I like your pyjamas,' he whispered, 'but I'd like you better naked.' She felt rather than saw his smile and he tucked the sheet over her shoulder, laughter lacing his voice. 'Sleep well, Chandler.'

CHAPTER FIVE

LIZZIE lay there, tense, thrumming, angry and afraid. Sleep felt very far away.

Yet she must have drifted off, for what seemed like only minutes later she was blinking sleep out of her eyes as Cormac exited the bathroom. His hair was wet and slicked back from his forehead, his eyes bright in his work-tanned face.

'Did you know you snore?' he asked with a wicked smile as he pulled on a crisp white button-down shirt.

'I didn't realise I had fallen asleep…' Lizzie mumbled, brushing a tangle of hair from her eyes.

'For nearly three hours. It's time to get ready for dinner.'

What with the jet lag and flying time, Lizzie felt completely disorientated. She didn't like the way Cormac gazed down at her, mocking laughter in his eyes, his whole body bursting with health, energy and determination.

He jerked his head towards a chair, where Lizzie saw he'd laid out some clothes. Her clothes.

'I want you to wear that dress tonight.'

She saw it was a simple green sundress with a white floral pattern and a halter-neck.

'I am capable of dressing myself, you know,' she snapped, but he simply ignored her.

He continued dressing, buttoning his shirt as he spoke. 'I talked to Jan while you were asleep and there's been a slight change of plan.'

'Oh?' Alarm prickled, nerves roiled. Change was not good.

'One of the architects on the short-list had to bow out.' He glanced at her; his smile had an air of triumph. 'His child was ill and had to be hospitalised. So you see where those family values get you.'

Lizzie didn't bother to reply. She knew any protest she made would be ridiculed. Reviled. Cormac Douglas was not a family man, which made this charade all the more difficult. Painful.

Ludicrous.

'So how does that affect us?' she finally asked.

'Jan picked another architect to replace him. An Englishman—Geoffrey Stears.' He paused, selected his tie and knotted it. 'I know him.'

Lizzie remembered what he'd said, how no one would know them. Of course, pulling this charade off would be so much easier with strangers. But if this Geoffrey Stears knew him... knew his reputation...

He might also realise he wasn't actually married. He might leak that information to Hassell, to the press.

'But doesn't that change everything?' she asked. 'If this Stears knows you...'

'Getting scared, Chandler?' he mocked. 'I knew you'd be easy to intimidate when I chose you, but I have to admit your frightened little virgin act is getting rather annoying. Unless you are actually a virgin?' He raised his eyebrows, the question in his eyes turning to a feral gleam before he continued. 'It's too late to back out, Chandler, so stop having second thoughts. There's nothing you can do. I've made sure of that.'

Lizzie's fingers bunched the sheet. 'How?'

'Or perhaps I should say *you've* made sure of that. You've played the game long enough for no one to believe you.' His teeth flashed in a smile. 'Your credibility is ruined.'

'I could still...' Lizzie began, and Cormac chuckled.

'Walk out of this room and tell Jan what you've been up to? Tell him how you've been tricked?' He pitched his voice in a contemptuous mimicry of her own. '"I'll tell her all of Cormac's secrets."' He gave a little laugh, a mockery of her own, before he shook his head. 'Tell Jan you've been deceived and he'll throw you out the front door. You're the deceiver, sweetheart, not the deceived, and you chose that role. So get used to it.'

'So now you're blackmailing me,' she stated flatly.

He shrugged. 'Call it what you will. I did what I had to to ensure your agreement. And you wanted it, Chandler. You liked the idea.'

Lizzie bit back a retort. What could she say except the truth? And she didn't particularly want to admit to it.

'Back out now,' Cormac continued, 'and you'll still suffer the indignity, the shame, or worse. Think about what that means for you…and your sister.'

Lizzie swallowed. The press loved Cormac. Loved to loathe him. News of his duplicity would be a carrion feast to them, and no one even remotely involved would be untouched.

The tabloids would circle her, devour her, then abandon her. Dani was eighteen, impressionable as Cormac had said, maybe even a little scatty. The results, Lizzie knew, could be disastrous. And Cormac must have known…must have guessed, at least.

'Don't threaten me,' she warned, knowing he didn't even have to. She was already so completely under his control.

There was nothing she could do. And Cormac knew it. Had always known it.

Had planned it that way.

'Like I said,' he murmured, 'enjoy it. Not many secretaries get a chance to live the high life in the Caribbean.' His eyes lingered on hers, flaring with possibility, with suggestion.

Lizzie felt an answering flicker in her own core.

She wanted this. Him. The excitement, the possibility. Even though it frightened her, *he* frightened her. Even though she didn't want anything to actually happen. Did she?

She didn't know anything any more. She was so, so out of her depth.

And he knew.

He had always known.

She looked away.

'You'd never say anything, anyway,' Cormac said after a moment, watching her with a little smile. 'And why should you?

Such a fuss…for what? Besides…' he shrugged into his suit jacket '…you don't like to make a fuss.'

'I feel like making a fuss right now,' Lizzie retorted. 'A big one.'

He raised an eyebrow. 'Sounds interesting.'

She flushed. 'Not everything has to be—'

'Oh, but it does,' he assured her. His eyes danced. She hated how she amused him. It made her feel so little. So unimportant.

'I may be attracted to you, Cormac,' she said quietly, her face heating, her heart beating, even though she knew it had to be said. She had to say it. 'But that's all it is. And I don't intend to act upon it.'

'Are you trying to convince me,' he murmured, 'or yourself?'

'I'm convincing you,' she snapped.

'I'm not convinced.'

Suddenly she couldn't stand his complete arrogance, his un-erring belief that she could be so easily known. So easily con-trolled.

'Maybe Jan isn't convinced, either,' she said recklessly. 'I could still tell him how you've blackmailed me. You waited until I was on the plane before you revealed your plans. I'm your sec-retary and you intimidated me.' She widened her eyes, fluttered her eyelashes. 'I didn't know what to do, I was so frightened…' Her voice was a breathy whisper and Cormac's face hardened, blanked dangerously.

Still, fuelled by a new, heady sense of power, Lizzie contin-ued. 'Somehow I think a man like him would believe me… empathise with me. Who knows, he might insist my name be kept out of the press! You'd be the only one hurt.'

'Is that so?' In one easy movement Cormac grabbed her hands, pulled her to him so her breasts collided with his chest, her thighs melded into his. She could feel every part of him pressed against her, hard against soft, experience matched with innocence.

His fingers laced with hers so that he pulled her even closer. Her breasts were now flattened against his chest, her belly and thighs and everything in between pressed against his. Even in her surprise and alarm, she felt the treacherous stirring of desire.

She'd never been so close to a man before.

She forced herself to meet his eyes—bright, sharp, cruel. He looked down at her, smiled with a parody of tenderness that made Lizzie's blood freeze.

'Somehow, sweetheart,' he whispered, his lips scant inches from hers, his breath feathering her face, 'I think you'd be the one getting hurt. Don't think you can play my game. Don't think you can ever use me.' His voice was soft. Soft and dangerous. Lizzie tasted fear.

'But you're using me,' she pointed out, her voice shaking. 'Just like you use everyone.' She tried to step away from him and, after a moment, his hands still easily encircling her wrists, he released her.

'Exactly.' He smiled. 'Let it go, Chandler. Just enjoy this weekend. I told you, it could be fun. Let's have fun.' His voice had turned to a caress, one she shrugged off.

'*Fun*? When you're virtually blackmailing me? You have a sick idea of what fun is, Cormac.'

He slipped his watch on, a tasteful sports design, clearly expensive. 'Blackmail's really a bit strong, don't you think? I might have waited until the plane to inform you of our plans, but you agreed. You said yes.'

'I never would have, if I'd known—'

'Known what?' Cormac took a step towards her. She could smell the cedar tang of his aftershave and tried not to breathe deeply. Even though she wanted to. Even now. 'Known what there'd be between us? What you'd be tempted to do? To want?'

There was challenge and knowledge in his voice and she didn't like, either. 'I'm not going to do anything,' Lizzie said, her eyes downcast. She wouldn't look at him. Didn't want to.

Couldn't.

'Good.' With two lean, strong fingers he touched her chin, tilted it upwards to meet his own mocking gaze. 'As long as you understand what this is about, Lizzie. It's not about blackmail. It's about power. I'm in control, and as long as you realise that, we're sorted. Understood?'

Impatience and irritation chased across his implacable features and Lizzie was conscious of a hollow, empty sensation, as if all her determination and defiance had leaked out.

It's about power. His. Only his.

She sagged, and suddenly she didn't care any more. Didn't care about the weekend, didn't care about him.

It was too hard, too tense, too humiliating and too *much*.

She just wanted this to be over, and it hadn't even begun.

She jerked her head away from his hand. 'Understood.'

She knew any threat of resistance or exposure was just that— a threat. Empty. She couldn't risk the shame and publicity telling the truth would bring. She didn't dare.

Cormac, she realised, had the power to make her life hell. And Dani's, too. And he would have no compunction in doing just that.

He might even enjoy it.

She turned to get dressed, stripping off her pyjamas, heedless of Cormac watching. Suddenly it didn't matter. Nothing mattered.

Cormac watched her for a moment, the pyjamas slithering to her feet, before he cursed under his breath and thrust her dress into her arms. 'Go ahead, use the bathroom.'

He turned away and Lizzie watched as he raked a hand through his hair, his back to her.

Bemused, she took her dress and underwear into the bathroom. She needed the space, the privacy, if only for a moment.

Inside the bathroom, she took a deep breath and ran a basin of cold water. Splashing her face, she forced herself to gather her scattered thoughts and concentrate.

She would not let him intimidate or control her. It was so hard—*he* was hard—but she had to stand up to him. She had to be strong.

Because, if she were weak, Cormac would take advantage. Every advantage. Easily.

Lizzie swallowed, resolve tightening in her middle. She could do this. She had to.

Dressed, her hair tumbled artfully about her shoulders, with a slick of make-up to help her feel better, Lizzie felt ready to face the world. To face Cormac.

She'd been shocked by his cruel statement of facts, his cold certainty that she was trapped. Shocked and even a bit hurt by the evidence of Cormac's brutal manipulation, his indifferent admission to such calculating coldness. Yet she realised he'd been warning her. *This is who I am.* That, in itself, was a kindness.

A warning she wouldn't forget.

'Well,' she murmured to her reflection, 'you wanted to seize life, you wanted the adventure. Here it is.' Smiling ruefully, she turned away.

'So,' she said briskly when she returned to their bedroom, 'do you think this Stears is a threat? To us?'

Cormac glanced at her, a flicker of amusement in his eyes. 'No one is a threat,' he stated flatly, 'to me.'

'Oh, stop being so arrogant!' Lizzie exclaimed. 'If there's a possibility of exposure, I need to know.'

'There isn't,' he informed her, 'as long as you continue to play your role.'

'I will,' she promised, an edge to her voice. 'No more second thoughts.'

'Good.'

If only she had some hold over him, Lizzie thought morosely as she slipped on a simple pendant, the only jewellery she had. Cormac had forgotten the little detail of jewellery, though it hardly mattered.

If she had some leverage, she would feel more in control. Less afraid. Then she might even enjoy this wretched weekend.

The trouble was, she had nothing. No power, no control. Cormac held all the cards…and he knew it.

'So how are you going to explain your marriage to this Stears?' she asked when they were ready to leave the room.

Cormac shrugged. 'I'll tell him the same story as everyone else.' He glanced at her sharply. 'And don't, for the love of God, compensate by acting like some doting idiot. Stears knows I'd never marry someone like that.'

'Who would you marry?' Lizzie asked on impulse, and he gave her a dark look.

'Remember,' he warned, 'I'm not a family man. I'm just playing one.' Tucking her arm into his, he smiled. 'Ready, sweet-heart?'

Lizzie tried to smile. It felt like bending cardboard. 'Ready.'

The sun was just beginning to set, turning the horizon a deep pink, the sea streaked with orange below.

It was a stunning sight and Lizzie paused in the corridor on the way to the lounge, Cormac coming to a halt next to her.

She breathed in the sea air, fresh and fragrant, a lover's caress. She could hear the lap of the waves against the shore, the gentle clanking of two rowing boats tied to a weathered dock.

A brightly coloured bird skimmed above the water before flying into the vivid horizon.

'It's beautiful,' she murmured.

'Yes, and this time next year, five hundred more people will be able to enjoy it.'

She glanced at him, saw the hard line of his clenched jaw, the way he gazed out at the sea as if it were another world to conquer.

'Do you think of everything in terms of your buildings?' she asked, and he turned to stare at her.

'Of course.'

She shook her head. 'It's an obsession with you.'

He gave a hard smile. 'A calling.' From the lounge there was a trill of feminine laughter and he took her elbow. 'Come on, they're waiting.'

Lizzie took a deep breath, steeled herself to begin the perfor-mance. At least she looked the part.

The sundress she wore clung to her curves before flaring out around her calves. It was simple, yet obviously expensive and well made. She even enjoyed the sensual pleasure of wearing it, something she was unaccustomed to. At least it was one thing she could enjoy this weekend.

She glanced at Cormac. He wore a suit in tan silk, the excel-lent cut and exquisite fabric moulding to his lithe, muscular frame. With his bronzed skin and eyes as bright as jade, he looked stunning, beautiful, his movements lithe and filled with an easy power.

As they entered the lounge, Lizzie was conscious of the conversation dying down and three couples turning to look expectantly at the new arrivals.

Jan rose and went to greet them. 'Cormac, Elizabeth! Come and meet our other guests.'

Lizzie smiled, aware of Cormac's hand on her elbow, his body next to hers, his strength and his heat. Everyone was looking at them as if they were a couple. As if they were in love.

Because, she reminded herself, for all intents and purposes, they were.

'I'm Dan White. I've heard about your work.' A friendly looking man with a wide smile and an American accent shook Cormac's hand and kissed Lizzie's cheek. He introduced his wife, Wendy, an attractive brunette who was quite obviously pregnant.

Lizzie took in her bump, Dan's protective arm around her waist, and realised how forced their own charade must seem. Standing in front of her was the real thing.

'Good to see you, Cormac.' A tall, lithe man uncoiled himself from the sofa to smile lazily at the pair of them before offering Cormac a rather limp handshake. His dark, sharp eyes took in Lizzie. 'Funny, I never heard that you'd married.'

'We kept it secret,' Cormac replied smoothly. His hand snaked around Lizzie's waist, drew her closer to him, her breasts brushing his chest. 'Didn't we, darling?'

'We did,' Lizzie agreed, and then surprised herself by giving a low, throaty chuckle. 'You know what Cormac's reputation was like, obviously, so I'm sure you can understand why we wanted to keep our heads down for a bit.'

'Indeed.' Geoffrey looked at her appraisingly, and Lizzie forced herself to smile back with a breezy confidence she was far from feeling. 'This is my wife, Lara.' He gestured to the woman next to him—blonde, feline and elegant, with a hardened glamour. She smiled, although there was no warmth in her eyes.

'Good to see you again, Cormac.'

Lizzie felt a *frisson* of alarm that bordered on panic as she saw Lara smile at Cormac with all too intimate a knowledge. Her grey eyes glimmered with seductive promise, and Lizzie knew these two had history.

Sexual history.

The thought both frightened her—a woman like this would sense a fake, a *virgin*—and, absurdly, stabbed her with jealousy.

She couldn't be envious of Lara. She wasn't actually Cormac's wife. She didn't even like him. At all. Yet the feeling was there—real, raw. Ridiculous.

'May I fetch you a drink?' Jan enquired, and Lizzie asked for an orange juice. Cormac had the same and she was reminded again of how he didn't seem to drink alcohol.

The next half hour was a blur of chit-chat and Lizzie was relieved to fade into the background as the men talked about architecture. Hilda chatted cozily with Wendy about pregnancy and babies and, after a short reprieve of silence, Lizzie found herself face to face with a smirking Lara.

'So, how long have you and Cormac known each other?'

'I've been working for him for two years,' Lizzie replied, mindful of Cormac's warning to stick to the truth as much as possible.

'And then you just fell in love?' The sneer in Lara's voice was obvious, as was the disbelief.

'Pretty much.' Lizzie took a gulp of orange juice.

'Really.' Lara sipped her own drink. 'Cormac never seemed the marrying type to me.'

'You know him well?' Lizzie didn't want to hear the answer, but she knew Lara would volunteer the information in one way or another.

'Oh, yes.' Lara laughed, a rich, knowing chuckle. 'Cormac and I go way back. Before Geoffrey,' she added with heavy emphasis. The meaning couldn't have been clearer.

'You had an affair, I suppose,' Lizzie said after a moment, and was gratified to see Lara look both surprised and discomfited. 'I know all about his women,' she confided, shaking her hair back over her shoulders. 'Not their names, of course, but I'd have to have had blinkers on not to know that Cormac is popular with the ladies.' She glanced over at him—confident, relaxed, deep in discussion with Jan—and felt her heart twist. Was he manipulating him, too? Of course he was. Just as he'd manipulated her.

She smiled back at Lara, a smile of knowledge, of power, of

confidence. Nothing she felt at the moment. 'I suppose he was just looking for the right woman, wasn't he?' she said. 'And now he's found her.'

Lara's eyes were like pewter as she stood up. 'I suppose he has,' she said coolly, and turned away.

Lizzie took another sip of orange juice. She felt dizzy, strange, and she wasn't even drinking alcohol. She thought of the words she'd spoken to Lara, almost wished them to be true.

He changed…for me.

Ha!

Cormac was never going to change, and she didn't even want him to. She hated him. Almost.

Except right now, glancing over at him as he talked to Jan, she wondered. She wondered just what drove him, what had flickered in his eyes like desperation, what made him…him.

Who was he?

No one you want to know, she told herself grimly, and turned to smile cheerily at Hilda.

She wasn't what he had expected. The realisation both surprised and annoyed him. He didn't like variables. Uncertainties.

He made sure he never had any.

Yet Lizzie, Cormac acknowledged with a faint frown, was just that. Unpredictable. One minute she was nervous, timid, easily controlled. The next she resisted, fought back, bared her tiny claws.

She was like a baby tiger, a kitten, trying to fight against the leader of the pack. At least, he thought, she was learning that with him she couldn't win.

Still, she required careful handling.

He turned back to Jan, tried to focus on his lengthy lecture about the island's history, the need to preserve it.

He knew all this already, had researched Sint Rimbert and the Hassell family so he could practically recite it all himself.

He prided himself on being meticulous.

Yet he hadn't been meticulous about Lizzie. He hadn't known her well enough to realise how she would disturb him, how he would desire her.

That had been a surprise—pleasant, but unexpected. He'd never considered Lizzie Chandler in a sexual way until he'd seen her in that grubby bra, looking defiant and vulnerable and strangely sexy.

Seduction was a weapon. Cormac used it well. It was an enjoyable line of attack, but he would have to choose his moment carefully. He had a feeling that Lizzie was perfectly capable of ruining everything simply because she thought her feelings had been hurt.

Idly Cormac found himself remembering how soft, how silky her hair had been, twined between his fingers. He wondered if her waist was as slender as it seemed, so that his own two hands could span it. If her breasts would fill his palm, and if her skin was as smooth and golden all over as it was in the parts he could see.

Lust, pure and simple. He had to be careful.

Someone laughed and Cormac turned to see Dan talking to Jan. Jan clearly approved of the American, the devotion he poured on with saccharine adoration.

Dan was playing the part, Cormac thought, and playing it well. He'd dismissed Stears as a second-rater, and one who wasn't bothering to charm Jan. Even his wife looked sulky and bored. But the Whites—they were a threat.

Cormac watched as Dan rested a loving hand on his wife's bump and she clasped her own hand over his. It was a simple, intimate gesture, barely noticeable, and yet the very carelessness of it made him realise how artificial his relationship with Lizzie really was.

They didn't touch each other with careless spontaneity, easy affection. Every movement was calculated, tense.

Fake.

If Hassell didn't guess, he had a feeling Stears would, and then he'd whisper it into Jan's ear. Even though he didn't think Hassell would believe such poison, he didn't care for the man to have doubts…especially when he planned to tell him later of their divorce.

It would be easy enough for a man like Hassell to change his mind, wriggle out of the contract. Make a mess.

Cormac took a sip of his drink, wondered again why it mattered so much. Why he'd taken this risk. He could have let it go. He'd let other commissions pass.

But not this one.

'So, congratulations are in order, it would seem,' Geoffrey murmured, moving to sit next to Cormac. 'Funny how quickly you married.'

'When you know, you know,' Cormac replied blandly.

'Exactly.' Geoffrey smiled, and Cormac almost laughed to think how someone like Stears could actually believe he had some kind of power. 'And I think I know.'

'You're losing me, Stears.' He spoke in a bored drawl.

'I wonder,' Geoffrey mused, 'if I searched in public records for your marriage licence, what would I find?'

'I'd love to see you explain such detective work to Jan,' Cormac replied. 'Forget about it, Stears.'

'I'm not going to stand by and watch a man like you get this commission,' Stears hissed.

Cormac swivelled to regard him with cold, blank eyes. 'A man like me?' he queried politely.

Geoffrey smirked. 'You've clawed your way to the top, haven't you, Douglas? You still bear the scars. I know people are impressed with your designs, your drive, but you don't belong. You never did and you never will.'

Cormac gave a slight shake of his head. 'People are looking, Geoffrey. I think you might want to calm yourself.'

'You'd do anything to get a commission,' Stears continued in a low, vicious voice. 'And I for one am going to make damn sure you don't get it.' He moved away on the pretext of refreshing his drink and Cormac watched him go, his lips tightening in resolve.

Geoffrey didn't scare him; the man didn't even bother him. But he was a variable that needed to be considered.

He glanced at Lizzie, chatting now with Hilda, watched as her slender fingers brushed at a wisp of hair. She smiled, and he felt a tightening in his gut.

He knew a way to silence Stears and his own stirrings. Glancing at Dan and Wendy, he knew he and Lizzie couldn't fake the real thing.

They could have the real thing.

Or close to it.

He could seduce her.

It might be just what was needed to seal this deal. Lizzie in his thrall, in his arms, would convince Hassell like nothing else could.

He smiled, suddenly looking forward to the evening a great deal more.

CHAPTER SIX

BY THE time dinner was announced Lizzie's nerves were starting to fray. The game was getting old. Every innocent question and remark sent her lurching upright, nerves jangling, heart beating desperately.

She was tired, hungry, out of sorts. She wanted to let her guard down, release the tension. Stop acting.

Yet she couldn't.

Cormac moved next to her as they entered the dining room, putting his arm around her waist, curving her to him.

'Not too much longer, sweetheart,' he murmured. 'You're doing well.'

'Don't patronise me,' she said under her breath, and he chuckled as if she'd said something amusing.

'The correct response is *thank you*.' He moved off to find his seat, and Hilda directed Lizzie to hers. She saw with a sinking heart that she was between Wendy and Geoffrey, and Cormac was next to Lara. Neither good options, both fraught with danger.

'The beach is so lovely here,' Cormac said as everyone began eating the first course, 'with a nice, shallow sandy bottom. Is the whole island so fortunate?'

Jan smiled. 'No, the north shore is rocky and quite impossible. The south side is lovely, though…' He paused. 'Where the resort shall be built.' There was a fleeting look of sadness in Jan's eyes and Lizzie wondered again about the reasons behind building the resort.

She glanced down at her starter, a warm asparagus salad with

Gouda cheese. It was delicious, yet she felt so queasy and out of sorts that each mouthful was hard to swallow.

Geoffrey noticed and murmured silkily in her ear, 'Not feeling yourself, Elizabeth?'

She glanced at him sharply. 'The jet lag has thrown my appetite off.'

'Pity.' He smiled, but his eyes were as sharp as a pair of scissors. 'Funny,' he continued after a moment, 'that I never heard of Cormac's nuptials. The architecture world is rather small in Great Britain.'

Lizzie felt a cold, plunging sensation in the pit of her stomach; she tasted bile. 'As I think I've said, we've been wanting to keep it quiet.'

'Very quiet.'

'Yes.' She took a bite of salad and realised it was a mistake when it stuck in her throat. Coughing, she gulped from her glass of water, conscious of Geoffrey's amused gaze.

'It's just rather convenient,' he said in a voice meant only for Lizzie's ears, 'that Cormac Douglas would suddenly get married mere weeks before this commission was announced. Don't you think?'

She shrugged. 'Coincidence, more than convenience, I would say. Besides, it's not official that the Hassells require a married architect.'

'We all know the truth...don't we?' The *double entendre* was too much to bear. Lizzie turned back to her salad.

Geoffrey watched her, his eyes glittering with thinly disguised malice. 'Are you very much in love?'

Despite her best intentions to remain calm, Lizzie could feel a humiliating flush steal across her cheeks and stain the delicate skin of her throat. 'Yes, of course we are,' she replied, but by the look of satisfaction in Geoffrey's steely eyes she hadn't convinced him in the least.

'Geoffrey, stop hassling my wife,' Cormac called lazily across the table. He smiled to take the sting from his words and Lizzie looked up, startled. 'I know she's beautiful but she's mine.' His eyes fastened on Lizzie and she felt the shocking onslaught of his possessive gaze as if he'd reached across the table and touched her. Undressed her.

'My, my,' Jan said. He sounded pleased. 'Consider yourself warned, Geoffrey.' Lara flushed.

The moment passed, the conversation moved on, and yet Lizzie still glanced at Cormac—his harsh, angular profile, the way he leaned back lazily in his chair—and wondered just how much he was acting.

I know she's beautiful… Did he actually believe that? Could she trust anything he did, said? Was anything real?

No. It wasn't.

It just felt like it sometimes.

The appetiser was cleared and the first course—Piska Kora, a dish of red snapper with garlic and lime—presented. Geoffrey, fortunately, was talking to Dan on his other side, and Lizzie tried to make polite conversation with Wendy.

Her mind whirled, however, spinning with new, unwelcome possibilities. It was obvious that Geoffrey was suspicious. It wouldn't take much for his suspicions to turn into cold, hard fact…and what then?

Both she and Cormac would be exposed. Ruined.

Lizzie toyed with her fish, unable to actually take a mouthful. Suddenly she was well and truly frightened. Frightened of discovery, of shame, of ruin.

She should have stepped off that plane and spat out the truth. Jan would have believed her then, but she'd been so intrigued by Cormac's proposition, enticed by the excitement. Cormac had used that, played her mercilessly.

And she had let him.

This situation was her own fault.

Nothing was real…except for that. The fear. The danger.

'Elizabeth, you haven't eaten. Are you well?' Hilda's question was of gentle concern, but it caused everyone at the table to glance at Lizzie's untouched plate, and Cormac gave her a quick, knowing look.

'I'm sorry…my appetite is a bit off,' Lizzie said. 'But it looks delicious,' she added lamely, flushing yet again.

'Perhaps the dessert will tempt you,' Hilda said with a smile. 'But don't worry, I'm sure you'll feel better tomorrow.'

Lizzie nodded and smiled, knowing she wouldn't. She wouldn't feel better until she was safely back in Edinburgh, back in her own home, her own job, her own *role*.

Bolo di Kashupete, a sweet cashew cake, followed the fish, and Lizzie forced herself to take a few mouthfuls. She had drunk half a glass of the rich dessert wine and found it had clouded her head and made her dizzy.

A mistake, she realised, as another wave of jet lag crashed over her. She couldn't afford too many more.

'Our gardens are lovely in the moonlight,' Jan said after they'd had their coffee. 'Perhaps the ladies would like to take a stroll? There is a bit of business we must discuss,' he addressed the men, and Lizzie knew they'd been kindly dismissed.

Wendy pleaded fatigue and excused herself to bed, leaving Lizzie to stroll the landscaped walks with Lara and Hilda.

The sea was only a stone's throw away, yet it felt as if they were in a separate world amidst the gravel paths twisting through tropical plants and flowers, the sweet scent of orchids and hibiscus heavy on the balmy air.

The night was alive with the sounds of the island, the raucous call of a macaw, the scamper of geckos and the frantic fluttering of dragonflies.

'You must love it here,' Lizzie said, and Hilda smiled.

'It's home. It always has been.'

'Do you think the resort will change it very much?' Lizzie couldn't help but ask.

'I hope not. To tell the truth, we have considered this resort because we cannot sustain the island's economy on our own without tourists. Ever since the sugar plantation failed, we've needed a new source of income.' Hilda sighed. 'It is our hope that a small, environmentally friendly resort will both help the islanders and allow others to enjoy what we've been blessed with... without changing things too much.'

And provide them with some needed income, Lizzie thought. You did what you had to do to get by, she knew. To make it through, to survive.

Wasn't that what she was doing now? Trying desperately to survive, to come out of this weekend unscathed, unsullied?

If only she could.

'Tell me about your wedding, Elizabeth,' Hilda said brightly. 'Cormac mentioned how quickly you were married—so romantic! Was it a big wedding?'

'No, very small,' Lizzie said quietly, conscious of Lara's silent, speculative glance. 'Just a few friends and family.'

'Very nice,' Hilda agreed. 'And you are hoping for children?'

Lizzie remembered what Cormac had said about starting a family. It was impossible to imagine. 'Oh, yes,' she lied. 'In time, of course.'

'Of course, of course.' Hilda's eyes were bright even in the moonlit darkness. 'All in good time.'

'What about you, Lara?' Lizzie asked. She was desperate to change the subject. 'How long have you and Geoffrey been married?'

'Six months,' Lara said in a bored voice. 'But it seems like for ever.' She laughed, a rather nasty sound, and Hilda looked uncomfortable.

What a strange group they were, Lizzie thought. Hilda had been happily married for forty years, Lara unhappily married, it seemed, for just a few months, and she not married at all.

'What about your sons, Hilda?' she asked. 'They're all married?'

'No, sadly.' Hilda frowned for a moment. 'They're all living abroad, pursuing careers. It's one of the reasons…' She paused, shrugged. 'Perhaps one day. It happened for Cormac, it can happen for them.'

Lizzie nodded, not trusting herself to speak. The guilt was overwhelming and she fought to ignore it. There was no point in allowing herself to be swamped in misery, despair.

The rambling path they'd been walking on ended in a little square, a fountain burbling in the middle. The moon cast a sliver of silver on the scene, illuminating the still figure of a man on a bench.

With an indrawn breath Lizzie realised it was Cormac. Alone.

'What a lovely spot for a couple to sit,' Hilda murmured.

'Lara, let me show you our wild orchids…' The older woman led Lara away, leaving Lizzie alone with Cormac.

'That wasn't very subtle,' she said with a little laugh, and Cormac looked up, his eyes glinting in the darkness.

'We're newly-weds. We need some time alone.' He spoke cynically, a darkness in his voice and, Lizzie guessed, in his soul—a darkness beneath that light, charming exterior, that easy confidence. A darkness she couldn't understand or penetrate.

She glanced around uneasily, conscious that Lara and perhaps even Geoffrey could be lurking in the shadows, listening. She moved closer to Cormac, sat next to him on the bench.

'Cormac,' she said in a low voice, 'Geoffrey suspects. He told me as much at dinner.'

'Is that why you couldn't eat a bite? You were as pale as a ghost.'

'I don't want to be discovered,' Lizzie hissed. 'You, of all people, know what's at stake.'

'Yes, I do,' Cormac replied calmly. 'Nothing is going to ruin this deal, Chandler. I'll make sure of that.'

'How?'

'I can handle Stears.' Cormac's tone was so coldly dismissive that Lizzie felt like shivering, despite the sultry night air.

They were silent, the gentle lapping of waves a shushing sound in the distance, the chirrup of insects loud in the stillness of the evening.

'You could have told me about Lara,' Lizzie whispered after a moment. When Cormac didn't bother answering, she felt compelled to ask, 'You had an affair with her, didn't you?'

He shrugged. 'So?'

'You could have warned me!'

'It wasn't relevant.'

'Wasn't relevant?' Lizzie's voice rose and, when Cormac raised one cynical eyebrow, she strove to lower it. 'Cormac, she's slept with you. She…she knows you in a way I…'

Too late, Lizzie realised this was not a good conversation to have—not now, not with Cormac, not when he leaned towards her and said softly, 'In a way you want to, Chandler?'

'In a way I don't,' she snapped. 'All I'm saying is a woman

who's been with a certain man can tell when another woman…
hasn't.'

'We could remedy the situation, you know.'

Lizzie stiffened. He wasn't actually…suggesting…they…

She swallowed. 'Very funny.'

'I didn't realise I was being amusing.'

She glanced at him, saw the glimmer of a smile in the darkness and wished she could see more of his face. Even then she
wouldn't know what he was thinking.

'You don't want to sleep with me,' she began, and she heard
his soft chuckle.

'Actually, I do. Can't you tell I desire you?'

'No…you're just playing with me. Flirting.' Suddenly she
desperately wanted that to be true. And didn't want it to be true.
She didn't know what she wanted.

'Flirting usually leads to something else,' Cormac murmured
in a low, languorous voice. 'Something more.'

'That isn't a very good idea, though,' Lizzie protested weakly,
'considering…'

'Actually, I think it's a very good idea.'

Lizzie swallowed, scooted a bit further away on the bench.
He was teasing her, toying with her. He had to be. She just didn't
know how to handle it. 'How did the meeting go tonight?' she
asked in a desperately blatant attempt to change the subject.

Cormac smiled, amused. 'Dan White is a strong contender,'
he admitted with a shrug. 'Hassell is so thrilled he's having a
child, and White's like a big, friendly dog, jumping all over the
place, licking and slobbering.' He shook his head in disgust.
'Hassell has made this weekend not about the designs, but about
who we *are*.'

Lizzie regarded him quietly. 'And you don't want him to see
who you really are,' she said.

Cormac's expression sharpened, his mouth twisting sardonically before he shrugged. 'Of course not, sweetheart.'

'Don't—'

'Shh.' Suddenly his whole face softened into a smile, a sexy
smile that had sudden need flooding through Lizzie's limbs even
as her mind spun in confusion.

He reached up, tangled a hand in the silken strands of hair blowing against her cheek and drew her closer to him.

'Shh,' he said again, and kissed her.

The feel of his lips—hard, unyielding, and yet so achingly tender—sent every thought spinning from Lizzie's brain. A part of her knew—had known, anyway—that someone must be watching for Cormac to do this. Yet, even as her brain acknowledged that fact, the rest of her body kicked into gear, flamed into desire.

Cormac's lips caressed her own, his hand drifting from her cheek to her throat and then to her breast, his fingers expertly, easily teasing her.

Lizzie gasped against his mouth, felt his smile. She'd never been touched like this, and even though she knew it was a performance—a charade—she could not keep herself from reacting.

Wanting. More.

Her arms wound around his neck, fingers lost in the crispness of his hair. She felt herself lean forward to press her breasts against the wonderful hardness of his chest.

Even in the softened haze of feeling she realised that someone must be watching this blatant, brazen display and she stiffened in shame.

She pulled away, jerking herself out of Cormac's arms, and looked around.

No one was there.

She glanced at Cormac. He was leaning back against the bench, a smile playing about his lips—the lips she'd just kissed. She could still feel the soft, salty taste of him on her tongue. In her mouth.

'There's no one,' she said, and he shrugged.

'I thought someone was coming.'

Lizzie's eyes narrowed. 'Did you really?'

He grinned. 'No.'

Lizzie shook her head. 'Don't play with me, Cormac.'

'But it's fun to play.' He rose from the bench in one lithe, lazy movement, reached for her hand. 'Come on, Chandler. Time for bed.'

Woodenly she took his hand and didn't even resist when he kept hold of it, all the way back to the bedroom. Her mind was spinning—spinning from Cormac's kiss.

And the revelation that would have been obvious to a woman with any experience—any woman but her.

He wanted her. Wanted. Her.

Her.

Why, Lizzie wondered numbly, was that so amazing? So flattering? Cormac had most likely slept with hundreds of women. She was just one more.

No. She would *not* let herself be notched up. She wouldn't... couldn't...

Except it—he—was so hard to resist.

It felt *wonderful* to be wanted.

Back in the room, Lizzie stood by the door while Cormac began to undress, unself-conscious as always. The shutters had been closed, the bed turned down, the soft light from a lamp casting shadows on the tiled floor.

Lizzie watched him shrug off his shirt, the desire from their kiss still pulsing through her. She leaned against the door, one hand on the knob as if she would flee from the room, from what she was feeling.

'Going somewhere?' Cormac asked, one eyebrow raised. He was bare-chested, his hands at his belt buckle.

Lizzie closed her eyes, then snapped them open. 'No...but we need to talk.'

'All right. Talk.'

'I'm not going to sleep with you, Cormac.' Lizzie blushed, lifted her chin. Cormac simply waited, his hands still at his buckle. 'I can't do this. I can't pretend that far.'

His gaze travelled over her slowly, resting on her still aching breasts. His mouth curved in a knowing smile. 'I don't think you were pretending all that much.'

Lizzie's blush intensified; her whole body felt hot. 'You're right, I wasn't,' she agreed. 'Before this weekend, I never gave you a thought that way, but now...' She shrugged. 'I've come to realise I'm attracted to you. As you well know. And,' she added defiantly, 'you are to me.'

'Yes, I am. As I told you before.' He walked towards her and Lizzie's hand tightened on the doorknob.

'Don't.'

'Don't what?'

'Don't come closer.'

He paused, took a little step. 'What are you scared of, Lizzie? Me? Or yourself?'

'Both,' she admitted in a raw whisper, and he spread his hands wide.

'I won't hurt you.'

Lizzie choked on a laugh of pure disbelief. 'Cormac, all you'll do is hurt me.'

'It would feel very nice at the time,' he murmured. His eyes raked over her slowly, purposefully, his mouth curling into a smile of seductive promise.

Lizzie shook her head, knowing she was convincing herself as much as him. 'I'm not into casual affairs. I'm not that…'

'Sort of girl?' he finished. 'But I'm sure you could become one.' He paused. 'Who knows what could happen, if we give it a chance?'

'Are you saying we might actually have a relationship?' Lizzie said in a voice ringing with disbelief…and damning hope.

Cormac shrugged. He took another step closer and his fingers trailed temptingly down her bare arm. 'I'm saying let's see what happens.'

'I don't want to.'

He laughed—a rich, indulgent sound. 'Yes, you do.'

Lizzie closed her eyes. 'You could seduce me, Cormac. I know you could. I…I find you hard to resist,' she admitted painfully, her face on fire. 'But I'm asking you not to. I'd hate myself in the morning…and I'd hate you. That can hardly be good for your commission.'

He stilled, then smiled, letting his fingers skim across her shoulder, over her breast, his smile deepening as he felt her react. He tilted her chin, met her tortured gaze with light, laughing eyes. 'Let me know if you change your mind.'

'I won't.'

He brushed her lips in a kiss that still managed to sear her soul.

'You keep telling yourself that, Chandler. Maybe one day you'll come to believe it.'

He dropped his hand and, as if released from a prison, Lizzie stumbled backwards. She grabbed her pyjamas, clutching them to her chest as she escaped into the bathroom to change.

She *would* keep telling herself that, she thought fiercely. It was the only way to make sure it stayed true.

Cormac stretched in bed and laced his fingers behind his head. His pose was relaxed, calculatingly so, yet a restlessness surged through his body.

A restlessness caused by both desire and dissatisfaction.

Lizzie wanted him. He knew that. And he wanted her…more than he'd care to admit.

It had started as a challenge; it had become a need.

If only she weren't so innocent…so damn *moral*, clinging to her virtue like some outraged virgin… She couldn't actually be a virgin, though. Could she? In this day and age? At twenty-eight?

She came out of the bathroom, dressed in her pathetic, shabby pyjamas, and he found his lips twitching as he asked, 'Hey, Chandler. Are you a virgin?'

Lizzie stiffened, betraying colour flooding her face. A twenty-eight-year-old virgin. No wonder she was playing so shy.

'Even if I weren't, I wouldn't sleep with you,' she said in a strangled voice, her chin held high, and he felt a reluctant flicker of admiration for her spirit.

'But think how I could introduce you to the pleasures of the flesh,' he murmured enticingly, just to see her flush intensify. 'The pleasures of love.'

She threw him a hard, heated look. 'But there's no love involved, is there, Cormac?'

He leaned back against the pillows, eyeing her thoughtfully. 'That's what you want, is it? What are you going to do, wait until marriage?'

'Maybe I will.' Lizzie lifted her chin. 'Or at least wait until I meet a man who loves and respects me,' she finished with cold dignity. 'You do neither.' She slipped into bed, her back to him, a sad, hunched little form.

Cormac leaned over and tucked the sheet around her shoulder. 'But you still want me,' he whispered, and she stiffened under his fingers.

'It means nothing.'

'We'll see about that.' He dropped a kiss on the nape of her neck, felt the shudder run through her body, and smiled.

Cormac lay in the darkness, listening to the soft sounds of their breathing. His body still throbbed and ached from the kiss they'd already shared, from the knowledge of her body, inches from his, tense and still. He could smell her scent, lemony shampoo and something else that was just pure Lizzie.

Pure lust.

He hadn't felt such desire—need—for a woman in a long time. Perhaps ever.

He thought of what she wanted... Love. Respect. His mouth twisted in sardonic acknowledgement. He supposed he could give her that.

If Lizzie were in love with him, Jan would never doubt they were a happy couple. Stears would stop his innuendoes, as well.

The commission would be his...and what an enjoyable way to achieve it.

His mind flicked over the possibilities, the problems. Lizzie would have to believe he was in love with her...for how long? How much? He needed to be believable. She could never suspect.

It was a risk, a challenge—the rush he craved. And now it was a need.

He smiled. He wanted her; he would have her, willing, in his arms.

Soon.

Lizzie sighed, and he could tell by her easy breathing that she was asleep. Knowing such respite was hours away for himself, he rolled quietly out of bed.

He took his sketchbook and pencils from his suitcase and, sitting in a chair opposite the bed, stared hard at the still, sleeping figure before he bent his head and began to draw.

CHAPTER SEVEN

SUNLIGHT was slanting in wide beams on the floor when Lizzie awoke. She lay still for a moment, listening to the gentle whoosh of the sea only metres from their bedroom, the call of a macaw and the rustle of the palms in the breeze.

She glanced over at Cormac and tensed, expecting to see him awake and gazing at her with that sardonic knowledge in those glinting hazel eyes.

Instead she found him asleep, and she shifted carefully on her side so she could study him.

He was a beautiful man. In sleep, his face was softened, relaxed, his thick lashes sweeping his cheeks, his mouth, usually pulled into a frown or a scowl, now softened into a half smile. His hair was mussed like a boy's. He had the beginnings of a cowlick, and it made her smile.

What had Cormac been like as a boy? She pictured him in a private-school uniform, prissy and pampered. It was hard to imagine. Perhaps his parents had sent him away to boarding school. That innate arrogance, the expectation of obedience came, she thought, from money. Money and power.

Her gaze slid downward. His chest was bare, pure sculpted muscle tapering to slim hips and powerful thighs, hidden only by a thin sheet.

He wore boxers, but she could still see evidence of his manhood and it ignited a traitorous heat inside her, just by looking.

What about touching…

She lifted a hand, stopped. She'd been about to touch his chest…to *caress* him.

Had she no shame? No self-control?

Then his eyes opened.

Suddenly Lizzie was aware of how close she was, her face inches from his, her hand poised above his chest. She dropped it back on to the sheet.

Cormac watched her, his eyes the colour of moss, clouded with sleep. Then the sleep cleared and was replaced with awareness.

Attraction.

They stared at each other, neither speaking, and Lizzie was conscious of how her body responded to just that look, her blood heating as if he'd stroked her with his hands instead of with his eyes.

Her hair fell forward, brushing against his bare chest, and Lizzie heard his breath hitch.

Still, neither of them spoke, neither of them moved.

She felt trapped by his gaze—trapped, tortured, tempted.

In a weekend of utter falseness, this felt amazingly real.

A bird called raucously outside and the shutter banged in the breeze.

The moment was broken. Lizzie saw it in the coolness that stole into his eyes, the knowing smile curving that mobile mouth.

'Had a good look?' he asked.

'Yes,' Lizzie said.

'Change your mind?'

'No.' She gave a knowing smile of her own. 'You snore.'

He chuckled disbelievingly and shook his head. 'No one's told me that before.'

'I didn't think your women stayed the night,' Lizzie threw back, and he stilled.

'No, they don't.' He paused thoughtfully, although something—not sleep—clouded his eyes once more. 'I don't think I've ever shared a bed with another person for the whole night before.'

'Me, neither,' Lizzie admitted, and he chuckled.

'That I believe, my little virgin.'

She scooted off the bed and busied herself pulling clothes from the cupboard. 'What are we doing today?'

'Jan and Hilda are taking us over to the building site. We'll talk shop while you ladies gossip, and then we'll all head to the beach for an afternoon of sun, sand and surf. Tomorrow Jan wants to see our formal presentations.'

'I really am just here as arm candy,' Lizzie said with a shake of her head. 'Whatever anyone says about family values.'

'Delicious arm candy, at that,' Cormac said. Somehow he'd sneaked up behind her while she'd been selecting her clothes and now he murmured in her ear, 'If only I could have a taste.'

'Don't,' she snapped, and he laughed.

'You're so easy to rile, Chandler. It almost takes the fun away.'

She turned around, one eyebrow raised. 'Almost?'

He grinned, suddenly looking boyish and uncomplicated. *If only.* 'Almost, but not quite.'

Lizzie grabbed the rest of her clothes and headed into the bathroom. She didn't like Cormac when he was charming. Didn't trust him. At his most enticing, he was also the most dangerous.

No, Lizzie realised, she *did* like him at his most charming— or even just a bit charming—and that was the problem. It would be so easy to succumb to temptation. To desire.

She climbed into the shower, let the hot water stream over her and imagined what that would be like. Feel like.

What would Cormac be like as a lover? Would he be commanding, authoritative, taking control with skilled, knowing hands? Or would he be tender, gentle, awakening her responses with a supreme confidence that didn't need him to be in control?

Lizzie shook her head, suppressed a shudder. She had no business wondering about Cormac, what he was like as a lover, who he really was. Not if she wanted to keep herself—body and soul—safe.

Yet she was curious. Curious about sex, curious about Cormac. Curious about Cormac as a lover…and as a man. What had made him the way he was? What would change him?

'The trouble with you,' she told her reflection in the mirror as she towelled herself dry, 'is that you've had no one to care about since Dani left. You're just lonely and you want someone to fix.'

The realisation sobered her. Saddened her, too. For the last ten years she'd given her life to her younger sister, had poured her emotions and her soul into Dani's well-being. She knew it was what her parents would have wanted, and she'd been happy to do it.

But now Dani—carefree, laughing Dani—was gone, happily tucked away at university, and at twenty-eight Lizzie was left wondering what to do with the rest of her life.

Whatever happened, the rest of her life, her personal life, would have nothing to do with Cormac, she told herself sternly. So her mind and heart and treacherous *body* had all better remember that.

She dressed quickly in white capris and a pale pink blouse—sleeveless, cool and elegantly simple. Since they'd be outside for most of the day, she caught her hair up in a loose bun, wisps curling around her face.

Back in the bedroom, she saw that Cormac had changed into khaki trousers and a dark green shirt that matched his eyes, deepening them to the colour of the jungle.

'Don't forget your swimming costume,' he said, and Lizzie mentally cringed at the thought of the jade bikini the boutique assistant had chosen for her—two tiny scraps of shiny material and a bit of string. Suddenly the thought of Cormac—never mind anyone else—seeing her in it made her feel horribly exposed and vulnerable.

Reluctantly, she fished the costume out of her suitcase and packed it in a canvas bag with some sun-cream and a hat.

Outside the villa, two Jeeps had been brought around the drive to take them all to the building site. Hilda and Jan were in the first one, and Lizzie saw Geoffrey and Lara snag the back seats of their hosts' Jeep, no doubt in an attempt to ingratiate themselves with the Hassells.

Dan offered to drive the second Jeep, as he was familiar with driving on the right-hand side of the road, and Cormac graciously agreed.

Lizzie managed a smile as he slid into the backseat next to

her, his arm going round her shoulders in an easy, thoughtless manner that she knew had to be cunningly calculated.

She wanted it to be real. The realisation hurt. She'd known this weekend would be dangerous. Cormac would be dangerous.

She hadn't realised *she* would be dangerous. Her body, her heart. Her mind, her soul. Unbending, unfurling. Wanting. More.

Wanting what she'd never had.

'Careful, Chandler,' Cormac murmured in her ear, his breath feathering her cheek. 'You're not looking very happy with me right now.'

Wendy glanced back at them, smiling, and Lizzie forced herself to smile back and pat Cormac's thigh in a perfunctory way.

Cormac trapped her hand with his own and kept it there, splayed on his thigh, too high on his leg for her comfort. She averted her head, unable to stomach the indecent intimacy.

Dan drove the Jeep out of the villa's landscaped grounds, following Jan along a paved track that cut through the dense jungle. Lizzie could hear the chattering of monkeys and macaws even over the sound of the engine.

After a quarter of an hour, they broke through the dense foliage and came to a rocky outcrop high over the water. Lizzie took in an awed breath, for the sight of the Caribbean shimmering with sunlight to the horizon was still stunning to her.

Cormac heard the little indrawn breath and slanted her a knowing smile. 'Beautiful, isn't it?' he said softly, and for once Lizzie felt he wasn't mocking her.

He even released her fingers and she dropped her hand into her own lap, feeling strangely, stupidly bereft.

They parked the Jeeps where the paved track ended in a pile of dirt and Jan led the party across the rocks to a flattened area that had already been set up with a table sheltered from the blazing sun by a tent.

Lizzie could feel Cormac's tension, his energy and excitement as the men sat down to discuss blueprints, dreams and designs.

Hilda led the women down a path through the rocks to a strip of white sandy beach below, and Lizzie saw that a separate vehicle had brought all the amenities for a relaxed day at the beach.

Spread out among folding chairs and towels, sheltered by

beach umbrellas, Lizzie tried to relax and enjoy the sun and sand. She felt as if she were drawn as tight as a bow string, every sense and nerve on alert.

'They won't be long,' Hilda said with a smile. 'Jan has already seen all the blueprints, you know. This weekend was simply a way of meeting the men behind the designs. That's what is important to us.'

And who was the man behind the design? Lizzie wondered. What front would he present to Jan? She'd no doubt he had something worked out, a façade to maintain. Had he ever shown who he really was to anyone? Had he ever been that vulnerable?

The idea was laughable.

Lizzie glanced around. Lara had already stretched out on a towel, glistening with suntan oil, in a bikini that made Lizzie's own skimpy one look modest in comparison.

In contrast, Wendy was sitting on a folding chair, one hand on her bump, looking hot and uncomfortable.

Lizzie smiled at her. 'Can I fetch you a drink?'

Wendy smiled gratefully. 'Water would be great.'

Lizzie found a bottle of water in one of the coolers and handed it to Wendy. 'A bit hot, isn't it,' she said sympathetically, and Wendy nodded.

'Yes. Dan didn't want me to come, as I'm only two months from my due date, but I insisted. This commission is so important to him. He's been struggling in a large firm, and this could really be his chance to break out.' She bit her lip. 'Of course, I'm sure it's important to Cormac, too…and to Geoffrey…'

'I'm sure every one of our husbands could design an amazing resort,' Lizzie said a bit lamely, for she was conscious of another fresh pang of guilt.

If Cormac hadn't insisted on his own way—and finding his own wife—men like Dan White, good, steady, *honest* men, would have a better chance at gaining such a prestigious commission.

If she hadn't agreed…

She was as much to blame as Cormac. No matter what he'd threatened her with, she could have said something. Done something.

She'd simply wanted an adventure too much.

And now she'd had enough, even as she wanted more. There was a part of her that longed to run back to safety, to the shelter of her former life. And another part—a treacherous, tempting part—wanted this. A life. Cormac.

She smiled again at Wendy and returned to her seat, trying to involve herself in Hilda's cheerful conversation about the resort and its plans.

The words washed over her, soothing sounds, no more than white noise. Her mind buzzed with questions. Questions about herself, about what she wanted.

Cormac.

What was she thinking? What did she want?

Change your mind?

No.

Finally, the men left the rocky outcrop. Lizzie watched Cormac walk over to her, smiling easily although his eyes looked blank, preoccupied.

'How was it?' she asked in a murmur. She glanced at Geoffrey, who was looking sulky, and Dan, who greeted Wendy with more concern than he'd ever shown about winning the commission.

'Fine.' Cormac raked a hand through his hair. 'Jan likes my ideas, but Stears keeps making remarks and I can tell they're starting to hit home.'

'He knows, doesn't he?' Lizzie said, fear plunging icily in her middle.

'Of course he knows. He can't prove anything, though.' His eyes rested on Lizzie for a moment and she felt their warmth, a radiant heat that matched the sun.

They both burned.

'We'll just have to be more convincing,' he said lazily. He pulled her towards him and she was too surprised to resist as he gave her a quick kiss. She knew it was calculated, a staged gesture, but it didn't feel like it.

For one blazing moment she was conscious only of his lips on hers, hard and warm. He pulled away and there was no mocking laughter in his eyes, no sardonic knowledge. 'Why don't you get your swimming costume on?' he suggested, and Lizzie opened her mouth to protest.

'We'll go snorkelling,' Cormac continued. 'The fish are amazing here.'

A treacherous thrill shot through her. She wanted to spend time with Cormac, she realised. She wanted to have fun. 'I'm not a strong swimmer,' she began, and he smiled, laced her fingers with his and drew her in for another kiss.

'I'll keep you safe.'

'Cormac…' Lizzie shook her head. She knew this wasn't real, it couldn't be real. He was just acting. Yet, she realised faintly, everyone was chatting or changing. No one was watching them. There was no audience.

There was just them.

Why was he doing it, then?

'All right,' she said, and gave him a quick, uncertain smile before she fetched her swimming costume and ducked into one of the tents set up for the purpose of changing.

She emerged a few minutes later, resisting the urge to cover herself as Cormac looked across at her, his eyes sweeping over, then resting on her body, heat and awareness flaring in their depths.

She joined the others, wrapping a towel around her waist as a sarong. She needed some coverage, some armour.

It did little good, however, for she was as aware of Cormac as he was of her. He'd taken off his shirt and wore a pair of navy blue swimming shorts, and even though she'd seen as much of his body before, she couldn't quite keep her eyes off him, taking in the hard contours of his chest, the tanned forearms resting on tapered hips, the long, powerful legs.

Every inch of him brown, beautiful, perfect.

Jan was advising everyone on the best areas to dive and snorkel, a pile of masks and flippers near his feet.

'Careful over by the rocks,' he warned, 'there's a bit of an undertow. Nothing too dangerous, but you should be cautious, especially if you're not a strong swimmer.'

First, however, they ate. Staff had set up a delicious repast on a folding table and everyone helped themselves to fresh conch salad, warm bread and sliced mango and guava.

The tropical tastes were new and tangy on her tongue and Lizzie dug in with gusto, the sun warm on her shoulders, the breeze caressing her face.

She saw Cormac watching her, a strange, speculative look on his face, and she wondered what he was thinking…feeling.

A few days ago she wouldn't have cared. She would have said Cormac Douglas didn't *feel* much of anything.

Now she wondered. *What?*

Lizzie turned back to her plate of food.

'Care to snorkel, Elizabeth?' Geoffrey had moved next to her when she wasn't looking and now stood above where she was seated, his cynical gaze resting on her cleavage. 'Lara's not interested so perhaps I could show you some of the marine sights.'

The last thing Lizzie wanted to do was spend any time alone, anywhere, with Geoffrey, so she felt only relief when Cormac walked over and replied smoothly, 'Actually, Lizzie and I are planning to snorkel together. That quality time, you know, is so important to couples.'

Lizzie nearly choked on a disbelieving laugh. Cormac talking about couples and quality time was too ludicrous to be believed.

And, by the looks of it, Geoffrey didn't believe it, for his cynical smile widened and he raised his eyebrows.

'Indeed.'

Cormac laced his fingers with Lizzie's. 'Tend to your own wife, Stears,' he said pleasantly, and drew Lizzie towards the beach.

'You shouldn't antagonise him,' Lizzie said in a low voice.

'I wasn't.' Cormac sounded supremely unconcerned and, Lizzie thought, rather arrogantly so. Didn't he realise what a danger—a threat—Geoffrey was?

'Geoffrey already suspects,' she said in a furious whisper. 'If he mentions something to Jan, we could both—'

'Jan will never listen to the likes of him,' Cormac said dismissively. He bent down to sort through the pile of snorkelling gear. 'The problem with Geoffrey is he thinks he can get what he wants by sneering and looking down his nose at everyone. I've seen it before. He's lost more than one commission to me, you know.'

'Is that why he's out for your blood?' Lizzie asked with a touch of acid, 'or is it because you've slept with his wife?'

Cormac only chuckled. 'Jealous, Chandler?'

'Not on your life,' she snapped, too quickly.

Cormac shrugged. 'I'm not worried about Stears, at any rate. He's too stupid to realise how you play someone like Hassell.' He stood up, a mask dangling from his fingers. 'Here, this should do nicely for you.'

Lizzie stared at him, suddenly feeling icy cold despite the blazing sun on her body. *How you play someone like Hassell.* The words echoed in her mind, reminding her that, whatever she thought—believed, hoped—Cormac didn't care about anyone. He played people...was playing her.

Don't ever forget it.

She shook her head. 'Is everyone just a pawn to be used to you?'

He cocked his head, his eyes vivid and alert, yet with a certain hardness to his face, his mouth. 'What do you think?' he asked.

Lizzie was compelled to admit, 'I don't know. I was beginning to think...to wonder...'

He stared at her and Lizzie saw irritation flicker in his eyes. He thrust the mask at her. 'Try this on.' He turned away to sort through the rest of the gear and Lizzie was left to slip the mask on—just one more layer hiding her from the rest of the party... and the man before her.

A few minutes later they stood at the edge of the sea, Lizzie feeling both absurd and nervous in her snorkelling gear.

'I'm not much of a swimmer,' she reminded Cormac, nudging the gentle waves dubiously with one flippered foot.

'Then we'll just stick close by the shore.' He reached a hand out, tugging on her fingers as a smile tugged on his mouth—and Lizzie's heartstrings. 'Come on, Chandler. I promised I'll keep you safe.'

She bristled even as she moved forward, reluctantly and inexorably pulled towards him.

'Why should I trust you?' she muttered, and his deepening smile went right through her soul.

'Because you can.'

It wasn't a reason. It wasn't even close to a reason, considering how he'd lied, cheated and manipulated his way this far.

Yet somehow it was enough.

The sea water was as warm as a bath as Cormac led her in, the waves lapping at her legs, the sand soft without being squishy between her toes. They'd only gone a few feet, the water just at Lizzie's waist, when he said, 'Look down.'

Lizzie did…and gasped. A rainbow coloured fish darted between her feet. Another silver fish, banded with black, slipped between her and Cormac. Lizzie laughed aloud in sheer amazement.

'I've never seen anything like…' she began, and Cormac tugged on her hands once more.

'Come with me.'

And Lizzie came, slipping into the water, following Cormac's lithe, powerful body as he sliced through the sea, his hand still firm on hers, keeping her safe just as he'd promised.

It took Lizzie a moment to accustom herself to keeping her face in the water, breathing through the snorkelling tube, but once she was she found herself transfixed by the underwater world opening below her and the man who pointed out each colourful fish, swimming confidently next to her, never letting her go.

She didn't want him to. She wanted this moment to last for ever—the easy intimacy, the sun warm on her back, its light dancing on the surface of the sea, a dazzling rainbow of blues and greens.

She wanted it to last for ever, even as she wanted more.

Why not? a voice whispered in her mind, her heart. A treacherous, tempting little voice. *Why not? You've had so little love in your life, so little affection. Maybe it wouldn't be love with Cormac, maybe it wouldn't even be close, but it would be something.*

Something she'd never had.

Something she wanted.

They swam all the way down the reef, amazed at the fish,

anemones and other small sea creatures, taking turns to point at each new discovery.

Finally they stopped waist-deep at a rocky outcrop out of view of the beach and the others. 'We should take a break,' Cormac said, slipping his mask and tube down around his neck. 'We've been at it for over an hour. You'll get tired out if you're not used to swimming.'

Lizzie slipped her own mask down. 'It's been amazing. I've never seen anything like this before.' She glanced at him, water glistening on his bare chest, tiny droplets clinging to his closely cropped hair, even his eyelashes. His eyes were bright in his tanned face.

'I suppose you're used to places like this,' she said.

He quirked one eyebrow. 'What makes you think that?'

She shrugged. 'The tabloids, I suppose. They're always going on about your jet-setting lifestyle.'

'Ah, I see.'

'Where did you grow up?' Lizzie asked impulsively. She wanted to know more about this man, more than the flickers and glimmers she'd glimpsed so far…or thought she'd glimpsed. She wanted to know about the man Cormac hid, the man underneath who was careful to leave no clues, no hints about who he really was, what he really thought. *That* man.

Cormac glanced at her for a moment, his expression thoughtful. 'Edinburgh,' he finally said.

'You did?' She was surprised.

'Yes, actually…' He paused. 'I lived in the house on Cowgate that's now my office. For a while.' He gave a little shrug and Lizzie watched something dark and fathomless flicker across his face like a shadow. A memory.

'But…' She trailed off. Twenty or thirty years ago, Cowgate had been a depressed section of Edinburgh, little more than a slum. Was that where Cormac had grown up? It was far from the life of luxury and privilege she'd always imagined.

A fish, as bright as a gold coin, darted between them. Lizzie laughed aloud. 'It's lovely!'

'Yes, it is,' Cormac agreed, but he was looking right at her and suddenly Lizzie was conscious of everything—the sun, as bright as a diamond in a brilliant blue sky, sparkling on the water, the water lapping gently against their nearly bare bodies and the closeness of Cormac, less than a foot away, water beading on a chest brown from the sun. How did he get so brown, Lizzie wondered hazily, living in Scotland?

'Don't look at me like that,' Cormac said with a little laugh, 'unless you're planning to do something about it.'

Lizzie realised she'd been gazing at him openly, hungrily, and she couldn't help herself.

'Like what?' she challenged, but it came out in little more than a breathy whisper.

'Like coming over and kissing me.' He reached out and tangled his fingers in the wet strands of her hair. 'I want you, Lizzie.'

'I want you, too.' She was dizzy, heady with the newfound power of her own desirability. Suddenly she realised what leverage she had, the control she could exert over Cormac.

It was herself.

Her body.

He wanted her…and it was about the only thing he wanted that was in her control to keep or give.

Or was it? she wondered as he pulled her closer and she didn't even try to resist. Didn't know how. Couldn't even think of it.

Didn't want to.

'Then come here,' he murmured, 'and show me.'

In a trance of need, she moved towards him—it was so easy in the water—until her breasts, barely covered in the skimpy bikini, brushed his chest.

'Do you know what you're doing?' he asked. He glanced down at her, amusement quirking his mouth, desire darkening his eyes. She heard his breath hitch and smiled.

'You know I don't,' she said, and kissed him.

Perhaps she'd only meant to brush his lips, but Cormac wouldn't let her get away with that. He pulled her to him, his hands lost in her hair, her body slick and wet against his. She slipped against him in the water until somehow she found her legs wrapped around his hips, his arousal pressing her in her most intimate place, a sensation she'd never felt…and she wanted more.

More. It was a flood of feeling, an overwhelming tide of need that scattered her senses and left her only aware of Cormac, his body, his mouth and hands and the need.

The incredible need. For him.

She pressed towards him and gasped as he responded. The water and their swimming costumes seemed very little barrier and something in her astonished response must have alerted Cormac for he pulled away with a muffled curse.

'This isn't… Come with me.'

Wordlessly Lizzie took his hand, followed him through the shallows, around the rocks, to a stretch of private, pristine beach.

In the distance Lizzie thought she heard a trill of feminine laughter, but it could have been the call of a bird.

Cormac kicked off his flippers, threw his mask to the ground, and numbly, hazily, Lizzie did the same.

The moment stretched between them endlessly, and yet it only lasted a second.

'Come here.'

Obediently, she came, stood before him. If there had been a choice, she didn't know when she'd made it. Perhaps there never had really been one at all.

He gave a smile of pure primal satisfaction before he took her in his arms and lowered his head to hers.

CHAPTER EIGHT

THIS was how he wanted her. Slender, glistening, perfect, her lips full and parted, ready to be kissed, her body open, willing, ready.

He smiled as he kissed her.

Her lips were soft, sweet, warm and hungry. She kissed him back with an inexpert passion that seared his soul and fired his blood.

Her hands stroked his chest, funny little strokes that weren't meant to arouse or entice. She was simply exploring.

But it worked. It worked very well.

Cormac lay her in the sand, warm from the sun and damp from their bodies. He wanted to be careful, calculated about what he was doing. This needed to be right. She had to feel…treasured.

He untied her bikini top and let it fall away to reveal pert, perfect, pink-tipped breasts.

She smiled shyly. 'Am I too small?'

'You're perfect,' he murmured, and brushed his lips against her breast, then found he wanted more. She moaned, her fists clenched in his damp hair, pulling her towards him.

'Cormac…'

Everything was new to her, wondrous and thrilling. He lifted his head, smiled and moved to the other breast. She arched towards him and he let his hand slide across her stomach to finger the top of her bikini briefs.

She tensed slightly, surprised as his fingers slid underneath the slippery material.

He kept his hand still, waiting for her to agree, to surrender as he knew she would.

After a moment her legs, taut with tension, relaxed, and she parted for him, letting his hand slide under her briefs to the very core of her, gasping as he stroked her with clever, knowing fingers.

'Cormac…' She moved, writhed, a stranger to the exquisite sensation she was feeling…*he* was feeling, watching her. It pleased him to pleasure her.

It was a new feeling.

Somewhere someone laughed, and he realised that even in this secluded cove there were people nearby. So did Lizzie, by the way her body stiffened and her eyes widened.

They stared at each other for a moment, Lizzie wide-eyed and searching, before the moment was broken, the wonderment lost.

Cormac rolled off her, his back on the hard sand, breathing heavily.

Lizzie was fumbling with her bikini strings, trying to make herself decent.

Around a tumble of rocks, two figures emerged. From a distance, Cormac saw it was Wendy and Dan.

Dammit.

'Hey, you two!' Wendy called out cheerfully. She glanced at their appearances, still rumpled, both of them stretched out on the sand, and blushed. 'Did we interrupt some private time?'

'Wendy,' Dan admonished. He grinned. 'They're newly-weds, remember?'

'Oh, of course. This could practically count as your honeymoon!'

Cormac chuckled dryly, ran his fingers through his sandy hair and smiled. 'We're planning a honeymoon eventually,' he said, 'but in the meantime, this will do.'

He glanced at Lizzie, saw her face was white and blank, and mentally cursed. The seduction he'd so carefully planned was shot to pieces. Now he had no idea how she might react.

'How do you feel the weekend's going, Cormac?' Dan asked. 'From what I can tell, Hassell has his eye mostly on you.'

'It's anyone's game still,' Cormac replied neutrally. He wanted them gone, wanted to take Lizzie back into his arms and make her believe in him again.

He wanted to repair the damage.

'Let the best man win, right?' Dan said with a wry smile. 'The best architect.'

'Exactly,' Cormac agreed with a small smile.

Dan glanced at Lizzie, who hadn't spoken yet. She was still sitting there, one hand fiddling with her bikini string, her eyes wide and dark.

'You look like you've had a bit too much sun, Elizabeth,' he ventured. 'Are you two heading back? I convinced Wendy to try snorkeling—I think we'll swim back to the beach. Everyone will be returning to the villa soon.'

Cormac paused. There was no point picking up where they'd left off—Lizzie was too shocked. Too embarrassed. He'd have to wait till tonight, in their room. More comfortable anyway, he decided as he brushed some sand from his shoulders. Then there would be no interruptions, nothing to keep them from each other.

Nothing to keep him from gaining her trust, her love, and enjoying it. Using it.

'Yes, we'll go back with you,' he said.

Nodding, Dan and Wendy waded into the shallows. Cormac turned to Lizzie.

'Come on, sweetheart,' he said, keeping his voice gentle. 'You do look like you've had too much sun.'

She gave him an odd look. 'You think so?' He held out his hand to help her up and she shrugged it aside. 'I'll stay here.'

Cormac bit back his impatience. 'You heard Dan. Everyone's getting ready to go back to the villa.'

She looked at him, a new coldness in her eyes. 'I'll walk.'

'Lizzie…' he warned, and she shook her head.

'No, Cormac, don't. Don't control me. Not now.' She stood up, brushed the sand from her legs. 'I'll see you back at the beach.'

Without waiting for his response, she headed down the stretch of empty sand, her pace resolute, her shoulders thrown back.

Cormac cursed aloud. He should follow her, he supposed,

make sure she didn't do something stupid like get lost or burst into tears.

Still, he didn't want to create a scene. He had no idea how she would react now, what she might do because she was hurt, furious or just plain frustrated.

This could, he realised savagely, cost him the commission.

But he was still going to seduce her. Tonight.

The sun was low in the sky, casting a golden sheen on the calm surface of the sea, when Lizzie finally found her way back to the makeshift camp. She hadn't realised how jagged the coastline was; walking had taken far longer than swimming would have.

She'd kept her mind blank, filled with the white noise around her, the soothing rush of waves on to sand, the call of seabirds, the rustling of the palm trees that fringed the beach.

It was easier to concentrate on those sounds than the memories which jangled and clamoured within her, desperate to be heard.

The memory of Cormac's lips on hers, his hands on her…

No. Her hands went up to her face and, despite her best intentions, the memories came anyway, rushed over her in an endless tide of regret and wonder.

She couldn't believe…

No.

Cormac. With *Cormac.*

She'd expected to feel desire, lust. But she'd felt tenderness, emotion, need.

And he hadn't felt anything.

Why couldn't it be uncomplicated? Why couldn't *she* be uncomplicated?

Why couldn't she give Cormac her body while keeping her heart?

She *knew* there was no feeling on his side. No matter how much she hoped or wondered. If he felt anything for her, it was casual, careless affection. Fleeting and fuelled by lust.

That was all it was.

Could it be enough? For her?

Was she willing to accept so little, simply because it was more than she'd ever had?

Lizzie shook her head. No. She wanted more, wanted what she'd told Cormac. Love. Respect. Marriage, even.

Nothing he was prepared to give her. Nothing she should want from him.

And yet...

She wanted *him*.

She didn't trust him. And she didn't trust herself.

Yet the want, the need, the hunger was still there, even as she knew that an affair with Cormac would lead only to more hunger, more need that could not be satisfied. Not by Cormac.

He wasn't interested in loving her. He didn't even respect her. And marriage was out of the question.

So where did that leave her? Nowhere, Lizzie realised with a grim smile, except exactly where Cormac wanted her...in the palm of his hand. Literally.

Cormac saw her as she approached the camp, and there was a look of thunderous fury on his face as he strode towards her, grabbing her by the shoulders and giving her a little shake before he kissed her hard on the mouth.

'Where were you? We've all been half mad with worry, thinking you were lost or dead—'

'I told you I would walk,' Lizzie said stiffly, her mouth bruised from his kiss. 'I didn't think you'd care.'

'I didn't think it would take you so long,' he retorted. 'I had visions of you trying to swim back, being caught in the undertow.' He sounded both accusing and anguished, and over his shoulder Lizzie saw Hilda smiling in concern, Jan looking worried.

Of course. This was part of Cormac's charade. He'd given her her cue, and was undoubtedly waiting for her response.

'I'm sorry, darling,' she said, and he relaxed a bit. 'I didn't realise you'd worry so much.' Or at all. 'Forgive me?'

'You'll just have to make it up to me later.' He gave her a wolfish smile and, taking her hand, led her towards the waiting vehicles.

Lizzie closed her eyes and let him lead her. For a moment she'd thought he hadn't been acting. For a moment it had felt real.

Never. *Never*.

The ride back to the villa was quiet save for the chattering and whirring of birds and bugs as twilight gave way to a cloak of velvety darkness.

By the time they arrived, everyone was tired from a day in the sun, and Hilda arranged for trays to be brought privately to the rooms.

She patted Lizzie's cheek in farewell. 'We'll see you at breakfast. All couples have their quarrels, no?' Behind Hilda, Lizzie saw Jan frown at Cormac.

The afternoon had cost him, she supposed, in credibility. God knew it had cost her something, too.

Lizzie managed to smile rather weakly at Hilda. She was not looking forward to enforced quarters with Cormac all evening.

Back in the room, he said tersely, 'Do you realise how dangerous that stunt you pulled was? Jan kept making remarks about how easily I'd managed to lose my wife, and Stears jumped in, saying maybe I'd never had her in the first place.'

Lizzie shrugged. 'You obviously made up for it with that little display of husbandly concern. Jan and Hilda looked thrilled.'

He paused. 'Yes, that was rather good, wasn't it?' He ran a hand through his hair and gestured towards the bathroom. 'You can have the shower first.' He paused again and Lizzie glanced at him, saw him frowning. 'Then we should talk.'

She nodded, surprised and a bit wary, before gathering her things and heading for the blessed oblivion of a hot shower.

Standing under a jet of scalding water, she wondered what Cormac wanted to talk about. No doubt he was afraid she'd read something into the afternoon, something that obviously wasn't there. She understood the afternoon had been about lust, and lust only. She didn't need a lecture.

Yet the realisation hurt. It was stupid, because she'd known all along and yet it still hurt. She hurt.

What would have happened, she wondered, if Wendy and Dan hadn't disturbed them? Would Cormac have taken her right there, on the hard sand?

Would she have let him?

Would she have been able to resist?

After her shower, she put on a simple shift dress in loose cotton. She exited the bathroom, combing her fingers through her damp hair, and Cormac didn't say a word as he moved past her to take his own shower.

There was a light knock on the door and a member of staff from the kitchen brought in a tray of food.

'Thank you,' Lizzie murmured, and glanced down at the makings of a delicious meal—a chicken dish fragrant with cloves and banana, cornflour pancakes and a fresh fruit salad. For dessert there was coconut cream pie.

She decided to wait for Cormac to eat, even though she dreaded seeing him, talking to him. She could still hear the sounds of the shower and suddenly the room seemed too small, too hot and confined.

Lizzie threw open the shutters and gulped in a breath of fresh sea air, tangy with salt and heavy with the fragrance of frangipani and orchids.

The windows of their room looked directly out onto the beach and, without even thinking about what she was doing, Lizzie swung her legs over the low sill, landed in a flower bed and took the few short steps to the sand.

She felt better out there, under a cool night sky, the air as soft and heavy as velvet. She heard the rustle of palms in the breeze, the lap of the waves and the sound of laughter from another bedroom.

She sat down on the sand, cool and hard in the darkness, and drew her knees up to her chest, her chin resting on top.

She didn't know how long she sat like that, her mind blessedly blank, but eventually she heard the creak of the shutters and then the sound of Cormac swinging himself over and walking across the sand.

'What are you doing out here?'

'Being by myself,' she replied, and heard him sigh.

'Chandler…'

'People might be able to hear,' she warned him in a low, terse voice.

'Lizzie.' Somehow her name on his tongue sounded so intimate. He sat down next to her, his arms resting on his knees. 'I'm sorry,' he said.

Lizzie turned and looked at him, surprised and wary. She couldn't see much of him in the moonlight, no more than the gleam of his eyes and teeth.

'What for?'

'For what happened earlier,' Cormac said.

She stiffened, shrugged. 'Sorry? That's not exactly a compliment.'

'It wasn't meant to be.' He lifted his hand as if to touch her, then dropped it. 'I took advantage of you,' he began heavily, 'and I shouldn't have.'

Lizzie stared at him suspiciously. 'This doesn't sound like you.'

He shrugged lightly. 'I'm not a monster…am I?'

'Sometimes I wonder,' she mumbled, and he stretched his legs out on the sand.

'I can't really blame you for thinking that, can I?' he said with a sigh. 'I dragged you into this. I didn't give you much choice.'

Lizzie raised her eyebrows. 'Don't tell me you're feeling sorry for that!'

He was silent for a long moment. 'No…' he finally said, his voice little more than a breath. 'Not exactly.' He reached out and tucked a strand of hair behind her ear, let his fingers trail down her cheek.

Lizzie tried not to tremble. Not to lean into his hand. Not to show him how much she wanted him.

He already knew, anyway.

He dropped his hand, gave an awkward little smile. 'Anyway, I just wanted to let you know that I'll stop.'

'Stop?' she repeated, and realised she sounded disappointed. 'Stop what, exactly?'

'Trying to get you into my bed.' He gave a little laugh. 'I want you, Lizzie. I want to make love to you. But I won't. I know you want…you need more from me.' He paused, and there was a tender uncertainty in his voice that made her mouth dry and her heart ache with both need and hurt. 'I just don't know if I can give it.'

She'd never expected this from him, and only now she realised how much she'd wanted it. Wanted him, his honesty and his kindness. Wanted someone looking at her, listening to her. Loving her. 'Thank you for being truthful with me,' she said after a long moment.

He inclined his head in silent acknowledgement. 'Shall we eat?'

She nodded, and he stood up, reaching a hand out to help her up. This time she took it.

Her mind spun as they headed back to the room. He helped her over the window ledge, smiled briefly with a self-deprecating humour that seemed entirely at odds with his careless arrogance.

Who was this man?

The real man?

The man underneath. She'd seen glimpses of him, flickers of something real. Something warm and vibrant. She realised now how much she wanted to believe there was more to Cormac than the ambition and the affairs. More than manipulation.

She wanted to believe in this.

She helped herself to the meal, then sat on the edge of the bed, her legs tucked under her.

Cormac sat in the chair opposite and dug in with gusto.

'This is delicious,' she murmured, trying to think of something to say, wanting to break the silence that had sprung between them, a silence of uncertainty, of possibility.

Cormac nodded in agreement. 'Tell me about yourself,' he said.

Lizzie looked up at him with an expression of patent surprise. 'Do you really want to know?' she asked, and he gave a little laugh.

'Actually, yes. I've worked with you for two years. I should know a little about you.'

Lizzie raised her eyebrows, still sceptical. Still afraid. Yet hoping…

Hoping so much.

'I thought it was your policy *not* to know,' she said, and shrugged. 'Besides, there isn't much to tell. You've already gathered the facts from my CV. My life has consisted of working for you and taking care of my sister. End of story.'

'What about your parents?'

'They died in a car accident ten years ago.'

'When you were eighteen,' Cormac clarified, and she nodded.

'Yes…Dani was eight. She was an unexpected addition to our family.'

Cormac took another bite of chicken, chewed thoughtfully. 'So what did you do when that happened?'

He actually sounded interested, Lizzie thought with disbelief. Caring. As if he wanted to know her as a person, and not just a willing body. 'I got my secretarial qualifications,' she said. 'Then I went to work for an architectural firm, Simon and Lester. Then I started working for you.'

'Was there no money when your parents died?' he asked. 'A life-insurance policy of some sort?'

'A small one,' Lizzie replied. 'Enough to take my course, and pay off the mortgage on the house. Then I needed to work.'

'It must have been very hard,' he said quietly. 'Going it alone.'

Lizzie stopped, her fork halfway to her mouth, her eyes suddenly, stupidly filled with tears. Why was he so understanding now? Why was he saying all the right things, when she wanted to keep her distance, keep herself safe…now?

Why?

Could she trust it?

'Yes,' she said, her voice little more than a whisper. 'It was.'

'Had you been planning to go to university?' Cormac asked. 'Eighteen… You must have given up your place if you were.'

'Yes,' Lizzie said, her throat raw and aching, 'I did.' How had he guessed? How did he know?

Cormac gazed at her for a moment, and there was an understanding in his eyes that Lizzie had never seen before. 'What were you going to study?'

'Graphic design.'

He nodded slowly, and they didn't speak for a few minutes. Lizzie concentrated on her food. Cormac's gently probing questions had brought back the old sorrow, regret for lost dreams. Yet she'd done the right thing. There had never been any question of that.

'I suppose there were no relatives to help out?' Cormac surmised. 'Or to take Dani?'

'No one was going to take Dani from me,' Lizzie said sharply. 'And anyway there wasn't anyone. My parents were elderly; they had Dani and me late in life. Our only relative is a rather dotty aunt we see on occasion.'

'So it was just you,' Cormac concluded quietly, and his tone made Lizzie want to fidget. He sounded as if he understood something about herself that she could only guess at.

'Me and Dani,' she corrected, and he nodded.

'Except now Dani's at university and it really is just you.'

She blinked, and then blinked again, horrified to find herself near tears. She opened her mouth to say something bright and brisk about new opportunities and second chances, but nothing came out.

Nothing at all.

'You've done very well,' Cormac said gently, 'haven't you? Even if no one has ever told you so.'

Lizzie tried to smile. She tried, but she didn't quite make it. She stared down at her half-finished plate instead. *Don't*, she thought. *Don't act as if you understand me, as if you like me, if you don't mean it.*

Don't.

Don't *stop*.

She'd never had someone who understood, someone who sympathised. She'd never had someone get close. And now Cormac was here, saying all the right things, doing the right things…but was he feeling the right things?

Did it even matter?

'Why don't you sell the house?' Cormac suggested in a brisker tone. 'Perhaps you held on to it when Dani was around, for stability, but now…you're an attractive woman. A young, attractive woman. There's a whole life in front of you.'

'It doesn't always feel that way.' She got up from the bed and dumped her plate back on the tray. She couldn't bear it if he felt sorry for her. She couldn't stand pity, not when she wanted something deeper.

'I'm sorry,' he said quietly. 'I didn't mean to offend you.'

'You just spoke the truth,' she said when she trusted herself to speak. She turned around, looked at him. He was sitting in the chair, his plate on his knees, a look of quiet, thoughtful compassion on his face that was just about her undoing.

'Cormac...' she began, and he waited. She licked her lips, tried again. 'Cormac...'

'Yes?' His voice was tender, filled with unspoken promise. Lizzie looked at him, the set of his shoulders, the way his mouth quirked in a smile, his steady gaze.

Who was this man? And what she did want from him?

She wanted something more, and yet something less. She wanted to feel, and not to think. To be touched if not loved. To just be...with him.

She wanted out. She wanted in. She laughed shakily, spread her hands out in plaintive appeal. 'You've said you'd stop, and I don't want you to.'

There. It was said. She stood there, quivering, waiting. Wondering. Wanting.

He cocked his head, eyed her thoughtfully. 'You don't want an affair.'

'Maybe I do.' And more than that, but it was a start. A start of something. Wasn't it?

'You'd get hurt.' He paused, and then said quietly, like a confession, 'I don't want to hurt you.'

Lizzie's heart squeezed, expanded. 'You won't.'

He pushed his plate aside, shook his head. 'Lizzie...' She didn't know whether it was a plea to stop or begin, and suddenly she didn't care.

'Don't. Don't tell me no when all weekend you've been wanting yes. Don't change your mind.' Her voice broke, and she sucked in a desperate breath. 'You've said you want me. I want you. I want to feel...' She shook her head, not willing to admit the truth.

She wanted to feel loved. Loved.

Cormac leaned forward. 'I just don't want there to be any regrets,' he said.

'There won't be.'

'I don't…' He raked a hand through his hair. 'Lizzie, I don't know how much I can offer you…the things you've said you want.'

'Love?' she asked in a wavering voice, and he lowered his head.

'I just don't know.' He lifted his gaze, gave her the ghost of a smile. 'We could just see what happens.'

Hope buoyed her lighter than air. 'We could,' she agreed.

She took a step towards him and stopped. That was as far as she could go. She needed him, wanted him to take control. To show her what to do.

'I'm rather new at this,' she said when the silence had stretched on too long, and Cormac gazed at her with dark, fathomless eyes.

'I'll show you,' he said, and moved towards her.

They stood facing each other, inches apart, quivering with awareness. Hesitantly Lizzie smoothed her hands over his chest. She felt the bump of his heartbeat against her palm.

'You see what you do to me,' he murmured, and a little laugh of surprise escaped her. His hand caught in her hair.

'Lizzie…'

'Show me.'

In one fluid movement he pulled her dress over her head; she stood there, naked, her skin washed in the soft glow of the lamp. Cormac's eyes roamed over her body slowly, taking in the small, neat breasts, the dark blond curls between her thighs, the fact that she was trembling.

Lizzie could feel herself shake; she was afraid. Even now. Especially now.

'You're beautiful,' he said softly. He shrugged off his shirt and trousers; in a moment he was naked. Lizzie's eyes widened at the sight of him—bare, bold, beautiful.

Hers. For now.

Easily, effortlessly, he scooped her into his arms, brought her to the bed and laid her down gently.

'You're sure this is what you want?' he asked, and she nodded. *Yes.*

He stretched beside her, his hands skimming her skin, teasing, toying, but she wanted more. More. She wanted deep, tight, hot, close.

More.

'Cormac…'

'We have time, Chandler,' he said with a little smile. 'Lots of time.'

His hand drifted lower, to the apex of her thighs. He cupped her breasts in his hands, kissed her navel. Moved lower. She shuddered.

He was wicked with his tongue—wicked and wonderful. She gasped as he touched her, tasted her where no one had ever been before, the very centre of her, melting with sensation…

She'd never *felt* so much before—piercing, painful, too much to bear. Too wonderful.

And yet…

'*Cormac…*'

'Yes.' She felt him smile against her middle.

'Look at me.'

He paused, and then Cormac kissed her again, deeper, his tongue so knowing, so clever…

She arched instinctively, her hands threaded through his hair. 'Cormac,' she gasped, 'I want to see you. I want to see your eyes.'

He stilled for only a second. Then, as if he hadn't heard her, he began his delicious onslaught again. She couldn't keep the waves of pleasure from racking her, a sweet torment she didn't want to stop.

But she wanted to see his eyes. She didn't know why, only felt. Felt it with an instinct, a deeper need than even what her body craved.

She pulled on his shoulders and, with a little laugh, he kissed his way upwards, his head bent, his face averted.

'*Cormac…*'

'Just let yourself enjoy it, Lizzie,' he murmured, his hand drifting down once more, gently stroking her. 'Let yourself go.'

Her body was desperate for release, but her mind resisted. So did her heart.

And still, she felt herself reaching the edge, teetering on it, her body opening, her breath hitching, her fingers clenching, everything straining towards that point…

'Cormac,' she gasped, '*Please*…'

Then a phone rang.

CHAPTER NINE

THE sound was unfamiliar at first, a tinny bleating that had Lizzie stiffening, then suddenly twisting away from Cormac. Her body still tingled with an unquenched fire but her mind was cold. Clear.

'That's my mobile.'

'Let it ring.' Cormac smiled, his hands reaching for her once more. 'Lizzie…'

She shrugged him off, icy dread pooling where desire had only moments before. 'No, Cormac. Only Dani has my number. Only for emergencies.'

He stilled, his face turning blank as she scrambled off the bed and dug through her bag for the phone.

'I'm sorry…' she breathed as her fingers curled around the mobile. Then she spoke into the phone. 'Dani?'

A hiccupy sob greeted her.

'Dani!' Lizzie's voice was sharp with fear. 'What has happened? What's wrong?'

'Oh, Lizzie, I'm in such a mess.'

She sank on to the bed. 'It's all right, sweetheart. Tell me.'

'You'll be angry…' Another pitiful sob.

'No, I won't,' Lizzie said firmly. 'No matter what it is.' It was a promise she'd always given, would always give. She would be there for her sister. Always.

Behind her, she heard Cormac shift. She felt him kiss the back of her neck and she barely suppressed a shiver.

'Come back to bed,' he whispered. 'Come back to me.'

Knowing how tempting his offer was, Lizzie moved from the bed to a chair. 'Dani, tell me,' she urged.

'I'm in trouble,' Dani admitted in a low whisper, and Lizzie's heart lurched.

'All right,' she said, striving to keep her voice neutral, matter-of-fact. 'What happened?'

'It was so unfair.' Dani's voice was high with sudden indignation. Whenever Dani was in trouble—for poor marks, bunking off class or being caught smoking behind the school sheds—she always tried to justify it. It wasn't fair. They didn't understand. It hadn't happened the way they said.

Lizzie knew she had sometimes been too lenient with Dani, not knowing how to act like a mother, feeling somehow guilty that Dani had been forced to grow up as an orphan.

'Tell me, Dani,' she interrupted her sister's mournful litany of excuses.

'I've been expelled,' she finally admitted sulkily.

'Expelled?' Lizzie repeated in numb disbelief. 'You've only been there a week! What on earth happened?'

'I was at a party…'

'And?' Lizzie drove a hand through her hair.

'I was drunk,' Dani continued reluctantly, 'and a friend and I got a bit…silly.'

'They don't expel you from uni for being silly,' Lizzie retorted sharply. 'Tell me the truth, Dani.'

'A group of us broke into the photography lab, meaning to take some pictures and well…a few things got broken. Expensive things.'

Lizzie closed her eyes, wondered how much they would be liable for.

'They're just trying to make an example of us,' Dani complained. 'It wasn't…'

'It sounds like it was.' Lizzie took a deep breath and tried to gather her scattered thoughts. 'I should ring the university—'

'No. I don't even want to go back.' Dani's voice trembled, and Lizzie realised just how young and afraid her sister really was.

'Oh, Dani. Let's not make any hasty decisions, all right? I'll be home in two days—'

'I need to be out of here tonight.'

'Tonight?' It really was serious. Lizzie sucked in another breath. 'All right. Well, you can take the train home and I'll be there as soon as I—'

'Don't hate me, Lizzie.' Dani began to cry, softly, and all of Lizzie's anger melted away.

'I could never hate you,' she said quietly.

'I couldn't bear it if you did.' Dani was crying loudly now, noisy, gulping tears. 'I know I've made such a mess of things. I've only been here a week—I'm sorry…'

'It's all right, Dani.' Lizzie spoke as if to a child. And really, Dani was a child. Her child. 'We'll sort this out.'

'I know you're far away somewhere,' Dani said with a gulp. 'But can you come home? For me? Now—as soon as you can? I…I need you.'

Lizzie's heart fluttered briefly with fear before grim determination took hold. 'Yes,' she said. 'Of course I'll come home.' Cormac would understand, she told herself. He'd shown what a truly sensitive man he was tonight. He knew about her situation with Dani. Besides, there was really only one more day left.

Her sister needed her. That was all that mattered…that had ever mattered.

Behind her she heard him move. Closer.

'I might be able to get a flight tonight,' she said, wondering if one of Jan's staff could take her to Bonaire. 'But it will be a while, Dani, if you can hold on…'

'Yes, I can.' She gulped. 'Now that I know you're coming.'

'Good.' Lizzie spent a few more moments soothing her sister, telling her to just get the train home and wait for her there, before she severed the connection and dropped the phone in her bag.

She looked up at Cormac and her heart stopped. The expression on his face was cool. Cold. Hard. He gave a tight little smile.

'What was all that about?'

Lizzie took a breath. He was bound to be angry, she knew. They'd made a deal. But Dani was more important. 'My sister is in trouble…' she began.

'At university?' Cormac clarified.

'Yes…apparently things got out of control at a party and she's been expelled.' Lizzie flushed. 'There's no excuse, I know, but she's young…' She trailed off at his cynical expression. 'Anyway, she needs me. I have to go home.'

'We have a flight booked in less than forty-eight hours.' His voice was mild, but Lizzie heard—felt—the steel underneath. 'Don't you think she can take care of herself till then?'

'She's a wreck, Cormac—'

'She certainly is if she's been thrown out of university her first week there.'

'Cormac…' Lizzie held her hand out in appeal. 'She's my sister. I need to be with her—now. As soon as possible. Jan will understand. He can get me a flight to Bonaire—'

'Those family values at work, eh?' Cormac shook his head. 'No, Lizzie. You're staying here.'

The cold finality in his tone went over her like a shiver. She stared at him, suddenly conscious that they were both naked.

'It won't affect the commission,' she said. 'I'll still pretend to be your wife—even wives have family emergencies!'

'Yes,' Cormac agreed, 'but how will it look if I let you run off while I stay to court this commission?'

'I…'

'It'll look like I care more about the commission than I do about you,' he finished flatly. 'I'm not about to have Jan think that for a second.'

'He'd understand—'

'It's not worth the risk.'

'But, Cormac!' Lizzie shook her head, confused. She felt that if she only explained, he'd understand. He'd turn back into the man he'd been before, the man she knew he truly was. The man who had looked at her with kind compassion, with exquisite tenderness.

That man.

'Cormac,' she tried again, 'I know it may seem unreasonable, but I'm all Dani has. She's my sister and she needs me. Nothing is more important than that.'

'Actually, something is.' Cormac's voice was frighteningly mild. 'My commission.'

Lizzie stared at him for a long moment. She looked into his eyes. How come she'd never noticed how cold they were? Life-less. Blank. And she'd wanted to see them. She'd wanted to gaze into his eyes as he made love to her and see love shining there, or at least tenderness. But there was nothing.

Nothing.

She took a step away and, suddenly ashamed of her naked-ness, she hurried over and snatched her dress, pulled it on with trembling hands.

'I don't understand you,' she said in a low voice. 'I can't understand how you can be so…so kind one moment, and then the next…'

'Can't you?' He stood before her, naked, unconcerned, arms crossed. One eyebrow quirked in cold cynicism.

Lizzie shook her head slowly. She felt dizzy, faint, sick. The man in front of her was like a reflection in ice, without a soul.

Frightening.

The truth.

'What's happened…' She stopped. Cormac stared at her. Waiting. 'You've been using me,' she said slowly, each word like a jagged splinter tearing her heart, her soul. 'You've been using me this whole time.'

Cormac said nothing, and the silence damned him. Damned *her*. Lizzie pressed a fist to her mouth, choked back a sob of hor-rified realisation.

'You've been using me,' she repeated, a disconnected part of her amazed at how well he'd played the role, how easily she'd fallen into his trap.

'All those things you said,' she whispered, remembering the words that had seemed so compassionate, so considerate, so… corrupt. Lies. All lies. 'All those promises…the understanding… the sympathy…you didn't mean any of it, did you? You were just saying what you thought I wanted to hear…what I needed to hear to get me into your bed.'

'As I recall,' Cormac replied in a voice of cutting precision, 'you were the one trying to get me into your bed.'

'Only because you made it that way! Didn't you?' She laughed, a broken sound of pain and lost dignity. 'You manipulated—*played*—me as you've played Jan, and Stears and every other person you've ever come across. So it would be my idea. My fault.'

'You're jumping to conclusions—' Cormac began in a hard, warning voice, but Lizzie shook her head. She couldn't bear to be managed and manipulated now. Not when she knew.

She *knew*. So much. Too much.

'You said you didn't know how much you could give,' she recalled, her fist still pressed to her mouth. 'I know the answer to that!' It came out in a cry, a cry of plaintive hurt that she choked back, biting on her knuckles, torn between fury and pain. 'You said you didn't want to hurt me! What a *joke*.'

There was a tic in Cormac's jaw. His face was otherwise impassive.

'What?' Lizzie demanded. 'Don't you have any more tricks up your sleeve, Cormac? Another way to manipulate me? You must have been laughing at me, how I fell for every soft, stupid line you gave me.'

'I was never laughing at you,' he said.

'No, you were playing me! Playing me like a fish on a line, and I *let* you…' She spun away, pressed her hands to her eyes, desperate to stop the tears. She wouldn't cry in front of him. Not now. Not ever.

'Why?' she asked after a long moment when the only sound was her own ragged breathing. 'Why did you do it?' Her voice came out stronger. 'What more is there for you to possibly gain? My humiliation? Is that what you want?'

'Lizzie, you're making more of this than there is,' Cormac said after a moment. 'What I said was true. I want you. You can't fake desire—'

'That's all it was!'

'I never said it was more.'

'Yes, you were very careful with your words.' Lizzie turned around, gave a sharp little laugh. 'Covering your tracks, no doubt. How long were you going to keep up the charade, Cormac? Pretending that you actually cared about me? Letting me believe that you were—different. Deeper. How long? About thirty-six more hours?'

His eyes raked her and he inclined his head, gave a small smile of acknowledgement. 'About that.'

'I was so desperate to believe you were a good man, that underneath that hardness there was—'

'There was what?' Cormac strode to her, grabbed her shoulders. 'What were you thinking, Lizzie? That this was *real*? That I'd suddenly fallen in love with you, cared about you?'

Yes. She stared at him, horrified, transfixed. She bit hard on her lips to stop herself from crying out.

'Yes, I played you,' Cormac gritted out. His eyes glittered with fierce determination, as if he wanted her to know. As if he wanted her to be hurt. 'I used you. I thought Hassell would be more convinced of our marriage if there was something real to it.'

'But this isn't real!'

'You believed it was.'

Lizzie wondered if she would be sick. She felt sick. Sickened.

'As I remember,' Cormac continued coolly, 'you were *begging* me to make love to you, no strings, no promises. You understood the rules.'

'But you were lying,' she whispered. Her stomach roiled. 'The whole time you were lying.'

'Did it matter if you believed it?'

She shook her head, closed her eyes as if she could blot his words out. Blot out reality.

This was Cormac. This was *that* man...so far from what she'd hoped. What she'd let herself begin to believe.

Cormac exhaled in disgust. 'You're pathetic,' he said. He released her with a contemptuous shrug. 'Look at you, Lizzie. Look at your life. Living in that mausoleum of a house, clinging to your pathetic memories of happy families, giving everything for your no-good sister—'

Lizzie gasped, but he continued, his voice hard, cutting. He knew the truth and he wielded it like a weapon.

'You've been so desperate to fall in love with me because you don't have anything else. Twenty-eight years old and a virgin? I bet you'd never even been kissed before this weekend. I bet you've never even had a man *look* at you before. I gave you clothes, I wined and dined you, I woke you up.' He bared his teeth in a feral smile. 'Consider it a favour.'

'You bastard—' She struck out at him, hopelessly, for he caught her flying fist in one hand, curled his fingers around her own.

'Exactly right. I *am* a bastard. My mother never knew who my father was and she taught me the best lesson I ever learned. Use or be used.' He laughed, a hard, ringing sound. 'And I am never used.'

'If I'd known—'

'And you were using me,' he said, cutting her off.

Lizzie shook her head in instinctive denial. 'No…'

'You wanted me to make you better. To fill up your empty life. It's in your eyes, Lizzie,' he taunted. 'You've been looking at me like you'd found a lost puppy to bring home, someone to cuddle and keep you warm. Well, forget it. I'm not here to make you feel better. I'm not going to fix your lonely, loveless little life.'

Each word echoed remorselessly in her mind, her heart. Lonely. Loveless. Little.

Her *life*.

He had no respect, no affection for her at all.

Nothing.

'Yet you pretended you were,' she whispered when she'd finally found her breath.

'No,' Cormac corrected, and there was satisfaction in his voice that made her nerves scream. '*You* pretended that.'

She stumbled away from him. 'You're going to act like you weren't playing me, Cormac? You weren't lying to me? Because we both know—'

'We both knew what we wanted,' Cormac stated flatly. 'And we almost got it.'

'If you even think—'

He laughed, shook his head. 'No, thanks, sweetheart. Too much effort for too little return.'

She stared at him, standing in front of her, naked and unashamed, with a supreme arrogance that even now he could use her. Control her. Bend her to his will.

'I hate you,' she breathed. 'And I'd rot in hell before I help you get *anything*—' In a moment of madness born of anger and despair, she strode to the door and wrenched it open, opened her mouth to scream, shout, cry—

Cormac knew what she was going to do even before she did. He reached her in two long steps and jerked her back into the room, pressed her against the closed door, his hand clapped over her mouth.

Lizzie's eyes were wide with sudden fear as he thrust his face near hers, his eyes glittering with rage.

'Don't, for a moment, think you'll ruin this commission for me now,' he hissed.

She tried to speak, to bite his hand, anything, but he only laughed. 'Lizzie, you might be angry enough with me now to think you don't care if you're ruined along with me, but you do. You do.' He paused, his restless gaze sweeping over her with cruel understanding. 'Think about Dani. Expelled already? And then her older sister, her mentor and would-be mother, gets caught in a web of blackmail and deceit? Goodness.' His eyebrows rose and his mouth curved in a mocking smile. 'That would look bad. That would probably send little Dani right off the rails.'

She kicked at his shins, fruitlessly, for he simply pressed himself closer against her, his naked length against her own body, and she felt herself respond even now, felt desire and need uncoil within her. She hated him. She hated herself.

'You want me, even now,' he breathed. And he wanted her. She felt his hard, sinewy length pressed against her, and suddenly she moved—he moved—she didn't know how it began.

She kissed him—he kissed her—a kiss of promise, punishment, their lips hard, bumping, teeth scraping, tongues entwined, each one pushing the other, demanding satisfaction, retribution.

She felt herself respond with a savage passion that roared inside her, a passion she hadn't known she possessed, a furious acknowledgement that even now she wanted him, desired him. Even when she knew what he really was.

And what he wasn't. What he'd intended her to believe.

She knew the truth, saw it with hard, hopeless clarity, and she still wanted him.

He broke the kiss first, pushed himself away from her and raked a hand through his hair. Their ragged gasps rent the still night air.

'You really are pathetic,' he said in a low voice, and Lizzie squeezed her eyes shut.

She'd never felt so low, so empty, so…unimportant. She'd been used and then utterly discarded.

And she'd let it happen.

Cormac walked away, pulled his boxers on and went to brush his teeth as if they'd just had a polite conversation. As if the world hadn't spun, shattered, and would never be the same.

Lizzie stared at him for a moment, watched him move with lithe, careless grace, untouched, untroubled by what had just happened.

How could she have ever believed this man cared—about *her*?

There was nothing beneath that charming, ruthless exterior, she realised. Nothing at all.

Slowly, with a little moan of despair, she slid down the door to land in a desolate heap on the floor.

Cormac stared at his reflection in the mirror. Adrenalin and anger raced through him. He braced his hands against the washbasin, took in a few steadying breaths.

It had been so close. So damn close. He'd almost had her, her heart in his hand, him inside her.

She'd believed every word, had been desperate to believe. To love.

He shook his head slowly. If the phone hadn't rung…if he hadn't dropped the mask for a moment…

He might have her still.

There was no question of that now. There would be no more pretty words, no more clever enticements.

She would never believe in him again.

He didn't care. He would never care.

He didn't know how, and he was glad.

He had to be. That was the way life was. It was better, he told himself, for Lizzie to understand the reality than live in a world of make-believe, a world where people cared about you, cared if you were hurt or sad, scared or alone. A world of false hope.

There *was* no hope, no healing, no one to make it better. There never had been, and there never would be.

That was the reality.

He cursed softly, and straightened. It was too late for regrets. Not that he ever had any.

Taking a breath, he exhaled slowly and opened the door.

Lizzie lay in bed, her knees drawn up to her chest, her eyes blank. She saw Cormac come out of the bathroom from the corner of her eye, but she said nothing.

His own words were reverberating through her mind, her soul. She took a deep breath, willed the waves of pain to recede.

Lonely, loveless little life. It was a cruel accusation, a bitter judgement.

And, she realised with stark, anguished clarity, it held truth.

That hurt.

It was painful to acknowledge, even to herself, like closing her fist, her heart, around shards of broken glass.

She'd thought she was happy. She'd *known* she was. Caring for her sister had been everything. It had been enough. She'd been satisfied, content, filled with purpose...

Hadn't she? *Hadn't she?*

No, she hadn't.

Not before Dani had left, and certainly not since she had gone.

Cormac had seen her emptiness, had known her need, and he'd exploited it. Without care, without regret, without any thought for her at all.

She had been desperate to believe in him. Desperate to be wanted. She hadn't convinced herself that Cormac loved her— she wasn't delusional—but a few kind words and she'd started to hope that he cared, that maybe, eventually, he could...

That she could make him care.

Well, she couldn't. She knew that now. Knew that he'd been able to use her so mercilessly because she'd been begging to be used.

She had asked him to make love to her. *Asked him*. Practically, pathetically said please.

She closed her eyes, too numb with pain to feel shame.

Cormac slid into bed next to her. 'Perhaps it's better this way,' he said in a flat, neutral voice. 'Now we know where we are.'

'We certainly do.' Lizzie's tone matched his for flatness.

'One more day and then you can leave,' Cormac told her, 'and I don't care what the hell you do.'

'Oh?' She forced herself to face him, to meet his cold, brutal gaze. 'But it won't end in one day, will it, Cormac? If you get this wretched commission that you're so set on. Because people will know; Stears will make sure of that. There will be an announcement in all the trade magazines…' She shrugged, actually managed to laugh. 'How did you think you were going to keep it up? For years, even?'

'I told you,' he said, irritation adding a bite to his voice, 'I'll announce a separation. A divorce.'

She shook her head. 'That will look suspicious. Don't you care what Hassell will think?'

'No.'

'Even if you have to work with him for several years?'

He shrugged. 'It's work.'

'It's all work, isn't it?' she said slowly. 'Just a means to an end.' She rolled away, curled into a ball. 'I can't believe I thought you were different. I was beginning to think you actually had something underneath all that ambition. Something real.' He was silent, and she felt his tension like a thin, taut wire through his body. Slowly she rolled back over to face him.

He stared at her, unmoved, immovable. 'I thought you were learning to care about something other than work,' she said, waiting for a reaction, hoping for a flicker of *something*. Something real, alive, warm. There was nothing.

'I thought when you said you didn't know how much you had to give, that you wanted to give more. But you don't, do you?' She shook her head, and her hair tangled about her flushed cheeks. 'I thought you didn't know how to love. I thought you wanted to be shown.'

Suddenly she felt unbearably sad. Sad for herself and her

own shattered dreams, sad for Cormac and the dreams he'd never even had. 'I wanted to show you,' she said quietly. 'More fool me.'

Cormac still said nothing, simply looked at her with those frighteningly blank eyes. After a moment, sorrow swamping her with the unending misery of their situation, Lizzie turned back over and desperately willed sleep to come.

CHAPTER TEN

WHEN Lizzie woke in the morning, the sun slanting in bars through the shutters, it took a moment for the memory of last night to come flooding back, and when it did she forced herself not to feel ashamed or angry.

Anguish came closer, but she pushed it away.

She forced herself not to feel. Anything.

She swung from the bed, resolute. She was not going to cringe and blush in front of Cormac. She was not going to think about what he'd said, what he'd done, what he'd made her realise and feel.

She wasn't going to think at all.

That was the only way forward now. The only way to survive.

One more day. Just one more day. She wouldn't—couldn't—think past that.

Cormac was still asleep, sprawled out on the bed, taking more than half the space. Lizzie spared him only a glance, knowing how dangerous it was to let her eyes rest on the sight of his bare chest, a sheet draped carelessly about his torso.

She rummaged in the closet, found a slim-fitting sundress in a vivid cerise. It was casual yet stunning in a relaxed way, and Lizzie knew it flattered her slim figure. She needed to feel good, and she yanked it off the hanger with a satisfied vengeance.

Behind her she heard Cormac stir, and she stalked into the bathroom without bothering to see if he was awake or not.

When she came out again, Cormac was up and half-dressed,

buttoning up a pale green shirt, a sliver of beautiful, bare skin visible. Lizzie swallowed and looked away.

'Are you finished with the bathroom?' he asked in a pleasant but cool voice. 'I need to shave.'

'Yes.' She reached for her make-up bag, studiously avoiding him.

It was a farce, she thought, this politeness. A veneer, a thin coat of ice that covered the deep, freezing despair below.

Yet it kept her going.

They didn't talk as they walked down the corridor to the dining room for breakfast. Wendy and Dan were both already there, along with Hilda and Jan.

Cormac had already told her that this morning's meeting with Jan was the most important, the time when the three architects would officially make their presentations. The wives were, for once, invited to stay, and although she'd once been curious about Cormac's vision for the resort, now she didn't care.

She was too blessedly numb.

The windows of the study were thrown open to the warm, fragrant breeze, chairs set in a row for the architects and their wives.

Dan gave his presentation first, his manner affable but a bit nervous, and Lizzie felt a pang of sympathy—and envy—for both him and Wendy, who sat with one hand on her bump, love and pride and hope shining in her eyes.

Lizzie knew nothing of blueprints or building designs, yet as far as she could tell it looked like a solid, dependable construction. Nothing too imaginative, perhaps, although she admired his determination to use local resources to keep the resort environmentally friendly.

Then it was Cormac's turn. He began to speak, his voice melodious, fluid, filled with passion.

He gestured to the plans spread before them, clearly having committed them to memory. He painted a picture of a place, a mood, an experience that had everyone in the room nodding, smiling and wanting it for themselves.

Lizzie watched him work his magic on the room, too disconnected to be wrapped in his spell. He was so good at it, she thought distantly. So good at using people, making them believe what he wanted them to believe. Making them feel what he wanted them to feel.

Use or be used.

'There would be hotel rooms for single guests and couples, bungalows for families by the beach.' Cormac tapped the blueprint. 'As you can see, the bungalows are designed with every amenity for a young family—connecting bedrooms, bath tubs and a small fenced outdoor area.'

'You've clearly been thinking of what a family needs,' Jan said with a chuckle. 'I can tell this resort means everything to you— perhaps you'll come back with your own family, eh?'

Lizzie didn't realise something was wrong until she felt a ripple of unease pass through the room in a silent current. She glanced at Cormac, saw he was staring blankly.

He shook his head, as if to clear it, and glanced down at the plans.

He looked lost.

'Cormac?' Jan prompted gently.

'I'm sorry…' Cormac stared sightlessly down at the lines and grids of the blueprint. 'Where was I?'

Lizzie knew he was losing it, had lost it, saw it in the faces around her, felt it in the tension and triumph vibrating through the room.

What had just happened?

'Perhaps this is a good time for my presentation,' Geoffrey said silkily.

'All right,' Jan agreed. There was an odd note of satisfaction in his voice. 'Thank you, Cormac. I think we've seen enough.'

Lizzie left the study with her mind still a haze. She didn't know what had happened in that room, in Cormac's mind. He had thrown his presentation—why? For what?

The architects were still closeted with Jan, and Lizzie decided to walk in the gardens. She needed some space, some air.

The gravel paths twisted enticingly through the thick foliage, frangipani, hibiscus, orchids and lilies drooping their heavy, scented blossoms on to the ground before her.

Within a few minutes the sounds of the villa were muted completely and she'd entered a world that was silent and green.

She found a small iron bench and sat down on it, her head falling into her hands. Above her birds twittered and called to each other and from a distance a monkey chattered.

After a few minutes she heard the crunch of gravel and looked up. Hilda stood there.

'Oh, my dear.' Hilda's smile was so compassionate that Lizzie immediately felt exposed, vulnerable. Raw. 'You've been crying.'

'No, I…' Too late she felt the trace of tears on her face. She *had* been crying…and she hadn't even realised. 'Sorry, it's been…'

Hilda sat next to her, put a motherly arm around her shoulder. She smelled like lavender and sunshine, and Lizzie barely resisted leaning in and taking a big sniff of that maternal scent.

'Is it Cormac? The first few months of marriage can be so difficult.'

'Yes,' Lizzie agreed in a choked whisper, 'they can.'

'It was a whirlwind romance, so Cormac said?'

Lizzie closed her eyes, snapped them open. 'Yes,' she agreed, 'he quite swept me off my feet.'

Hilda smiled. 'Understandable, of course. He's a handsome man. And very charismatic.'

'Yes.' It was the image he projected, Lizzie knew. Charming, confident, relaxed. That tactic worked with the Hassells. That was how he played them.

'Jan is so impressed with him, with his dedication to his work,' Hilda continued. 'When Cormac told him he was married, we were so pleased! To tell you the truth…' she lowered her voice a bit, although there was no one to hear '…Jan has always wanted Cormac to design the resort. But we feel strongly about the architect sharing our values…the values we want for this resort. It's important—special—to us.'

Lizzie nodded. 'Yes, of course.'

'Jan knew of Cormac's reputation,' Hilda continued, hastening to add, 'as an architect, I mean. Brilliant, but ruthless. Cold.'

Lizzie nodded again.

'He's had his doubts, of course. Before this weekend, he even wondered if Cormac was perpetrating some terrible ruse! Mr Stears had said something, and it was so strange, how quickly he married. But now that we've met you, and seen you…' She smiled. 'He obviously adores you.' This time Lizzie could not make herself nod.

'It's in the way he looks at you, even when you don't notice. And today—during the presentation—there couldn't have been a person in that room who didn't see how he loves you. Just the thought of having children one day sent him spinning. I think Jan was secretly delighted, even if the other architects consider it a misstep.'

'Is that right?' Lizzie's heart was leaden. Had that moment been planned? Faked?

Lizzie knew it was possible. Probable. He was a master of those kinds of moments.

She knew it all too well.

'Love conquers all, doesn't it?' Hilda concluded happily. 'It softens even the hardest of hearts.'

Lizzie's mouth was so dry she could not form or utter a single word. Hilda was clearly expecting some kind of response, so she stretched her lips into a smile.

She felt as if she might be sick. She averted her head and blinked back tears. Her mind was numb, her body drained.

I can't do this any more. It was too much—the pretence, the deceit, the desire, the rejection.

After ten stagnant years of little interaction or intimacy, this weekend was an emotional overload.

She wanted to go back to the way things had been, and yet at the same time she dreaded it—the return to her empty life, to the loneliness she hadn't even realised had been consuming her, swallowing her whole.

A life without Cormac.

When Hilda finally left her alone, Lizzie escaped to her room, claiming she wanted to nap.

She lay on the bed, dry-eyed and far from sleep, longing only to be home, for all this to be over.

She wrapped her arms around herself, closed her eyes and

found herself rocking a little bit, as if she were a child who needed to be soothed to sleep.

She wanted to sleep, to forget, but she couldn't. The thoughts, the realisations came instead.

She was used to loving. To giving—giving everything until you were empty, drained. Used up. She wasn't, she realised, used to being loved back.

Dani had needed her, had expected her to be there with open arms, listening ears. Dani loved her, of course she did, the selfish love of a child in need of gratification, attention, acceptance.

She wanted the love of a man. Deep, consuming, lasting. Real.

Real.

She'd looked to Cormac—*Cormac*!—to give it to her.

How foolish. How naïve.

How stupid.

Was it because he was the only man who had ever shown her even the barest interest? Or was it the man himself?

The glimmers of something deeper that she'd thought she'd seen, had so desperately wanted to believe in…

False. All false. Cormac would say as much himself. He already had.

The sun moved in a golden ball across the sky; its beams slanted more widely across the floor, the shadows lengthening. The fan spun lazily and the air was hot and still. Even the ocean's roar seem muted.

If only she could stay numb for ever.

The door opened and Cormac entered, giving her a cursory glance. 'You need to get up,' he said flatly. 'There's a dinner and dancing tonight on the beach. A celebration.'

'Did you get the commission?' Her voice was a lifeless monotone.

'I think so.' He shrugged off his jacket and gave a chuckle of satisfaction. 'It'll all be worth it, then.'

His words penetrated slowly, piercing the fog of numb misery that had surrounded and protected her for the last twenty-four hours.

'Worth it?' she repeated. She rolled into a sitting position, stared at him; he had a faint look of perplexity on his face. '*Worth it?*' she said again, and then she began to laugh.

Cormac stared at her, utterly nonplussed, as she laughed. Deep belly laughs that made her stomach hurt and tears roll down her face until she wasn't laughing any more, she was crying.

Sobbing in a way she never had, in a way she'd never let herself. Hard, wrenching gasps of agonised feeling, tears running unchecked down her face, her nose running, her face red and blotched.

She didn't even know why she was crying—for Cormac, for herself, for the problem with Dani, for the last ten years when she'd given so much of herself that she wasn't sure what was left or who she was any more…and she hadn't realised *that* until Cormac had shown her. Told her.

Used her.

Now she felt, felt it all in a tide of feeling that she'd kept at bay for too long. It rushed over her, drowned her, and still, she sobbed.

She was aware, dimly, that Cormac was simply watching her, his face as blank as ever. He looked almost bored.

'Are you about done?' he asked when she'd drawn in a last shuddering breath.

Lizzie looked up at him, aware that she'd bared more to this man than to anyone in her entire life. And he didn't care. He didn't want her.

He thought she was pathetic.

And maybe she was.

She laughed, although it came out as one last hiccuppy sob. It was simply all too horrible.

'Yes,' she said, wiping her wet cheeks, 'I'm done.'

'Good. You have half an hour to get ready.' Cormac strode into the bathroom.

Lizzie sank back against the pillows, exhausted yet also somehow sated. 'Yes,' she said aloud to the empty room, 'I'm done.'

She looked marginally better than a corpse, she decided as they made their way to the beach. The silver evening gown clung and swirled about her; it was a beautiful dress. Her hair streamed over her shoulders like gilt in the moonlight, but her face was pale, pinched, drawn in lines of misery.

Next to her, Cormac was devastating in a tuxedo, the pure whiteness of his evening shirt highlighting his tanned skin, his eyes glittering like jade in the darkness.

He held out his arm and wordlessly Lizzie took it. She felt like a doll—lifeless, emotionless, performing the wretched part.

Soon it will be over.

Soon.

The beach had been transformed into something like a fairy grotto, Lizzie saw, as they approached the party via the gravel path twisting through landscaped gardens.

Tables flickering with candlelight and crystal had been set up on a platform and fairy lights were entwined in the palm trees. Tiki torches enclosed the space with warm light and she could hear the strains of Caribbean music, steel drums and a guitar coming from a wooden dais.

Metres away the ocean shushed a soothing, rhythmic lullaby.

The other guests were assembled, including some local residents and staff Lizzie had not met.

Lara, she saw, wore a skimpy but stylish black number, and Wendy was looking cumbersome and self-conscious in a floaty dress that did nothing to disguise her bump. Dan had his arm around his wife in a protective manner, and Lizzie felt a lump in her throat at the sight.

Wendy had clearly had a difficult time this weekend, with the fatigue and heat, and Dan was aware and protecting her.

She'd had a difficult time, too, she thought with a soundless laugh, and look how Cormac treated her. He'd *caused* it.

Then she realised with an odd little jolt that Cormac *did* have his arm around her.

Only to show everyone what a loving husband he was, she knew, only for pretend. It shouldn't have hurt, not now, when she knew—she *knew* the way things were.

And the way things weren't.

She couldn't bear it. She couldn't bear any more.

Cormac must have sensed her thoughts, her tension, for he looked down and said, 'What is it?'

Lizzie just shook her head and moved towards the lights.

'Elizabeth, so glad you joined us.' Smiling, Jan came forward and kissed both her cheeks. 'Hilda said you weren't feeling well earlier,' he continued in a low voice, 'but I trust that has passed? You look lovely.'

She forced herself to smile. 'I think I was just tired from all that sun yesterday.'

Jan squeezed her hand. 'Good. I'm so glad, my dear. So happy for you both.' He glanced across at Cormac, who had gone to the makeshift bar to fetch them drinks. 'I was very impressed with your husband's work this morning, despite his little misstep. Do you know, he told me later it was concern for you that caused him to forget his presentation, and I was heartened by that…as perhaps you should be?'

Jan's smile was gentle, compassionate and far too understanding.

Lizzie tried to speak and found there was nothing to say. Jan had just as good as told her that Cormac's hesitation had been planned, as she'd suspected. Feared. How had he known that Jan would react that way?

He was good, she knew, at reading people. At reading her. And he always, *always* used it to his advantage.

'Here we are.' Smiling easily, Cormac handed her a creamy, fruity drink and took a sip of his own fruit juice.

'Cormac, your wife looks ravishing tonight,' Jan said. 'I was just telling her so.'

'Indeed, she does.' Still smiling, Cormac put his arm around Lizzie and drew her to his side. His fingers gently stroked her bare arm and even now desire pooled in her middle at the slight, seductive sensation of his fingers.

Jan saw the movement and couldn't help but beam. 'So in love…' he approved. 'It's a wonderful thing to see.'

Cormac smiled and gave a little chuckle of acknowledgement and thanks even as he squeezed Lizzie's shoulder in warning.

The pretence, the parody made her nerves jangle, scream.

She couldn't stand another moment of Jan's innocent, smiling joviality or Cormac's fake adoration.

'Excuse me,' she murmured and, heedless of what consternation she caused, she left the two men and headed for a quiet corner of the party.

Cormac joined her a few minutes later. 'That was a close one, Chandler.'

'I don't care.'

'Well, you should,' he replied in a low snarl. 'Do you recall what could happen to both of us if our little charade is discovered?'

'Yes, I have,' Lizzie replied. 'I just don't care any more.'

'What about your sister—?'

She shook her head. 'I don't care, Cormac. I don't care. Stop playing your damn trump cards. I'll act as best I can, I won't ruin your precious charade because it's too much effort now but understand this.' She looked at him, her face hard, as blank and determined as his own. '*I don't care.*'

'Good.' He stared at her, his gaze just as hard. Harder. 'If only it had been that way all along.'

CHAPTER ELEVEN

IT WAS raining as the plane landed in Edinburgh.

Lizzie stared out at the drizzly night sky and decided that the weather matched her mood exactly. Damp, grey, leaden.

At least the pretence was over. She'd tried to comfort herself with this thought during the interminable hours of their flight, but derived little solace from the knowledge.

They'd barely spoken a word since boarding the plane on Bonaire. As soon as the pilot from Sint Rimbert had waved goodbye, Cormac had dropped the mask of loving husband and discarded it without a thought.

He had no use for pretence any more.

He had no use for her.

He'd immersed himself in work the entire flight, shielding her gaze from what looked like a sketchbook, and Lizzie imagined he was designing new plans for the resort. She hadn't been able to summon either the energy or the courage to even ask if he'd officially been given the commission.

She didn't care; she cared too much.

She'd stared out of the window instead, had pretended to sleep. Had worked hard at avoiding Cormac right next to her, acted like it didn't matter.

It shouldn't matter. The wretched charade was over and her life could return to normal.

The new normal, she thought despondently. Nothing felt like it would ever be *normal* again.

She sighed, leaned her head against the back of the seat as the plane taxied to a stop.

'A car is picking me up,' Cormac informed her as he put his sketchbook back into his attaché case. 'You can share it if you like.'

Lizzie hesitated. The idea of more enforced quarters with Cormac was unappealing, but so was a taxi or bus ride into the city with all of her bags.

'Thank you,' she said, and Cormac merely nodded before turning back to his work.

They maintained a curt silence in the car on the way home, rain sluicing against the windows, the lights of the traffic nothing more than bright, blurry shapes.

Lizzie was relieved to see the darkened form of her town house. It was after midnight and she supposed that Dani, having arrived yesterday, was asleep.

'Take the day off tomorrow,' Cormac informed her as the car pulled to a stop. 'I'll leave work for you in the office. I'll be in London for the next few weeks.'

'You will?' She felt both disappointed and relieved. His announcement was neither unexpected nor unusual. Cormac often went to London for weeks at a time. 'All right, then.' She glanced at him, wanting to say something, anything—why?

To acknowledge all that had happened that weekend, all she'd felt, experienced, *hoped*. All that she'd suffered and lost.

She wanted something from him, even now, even if it was only an insincere apology.

There was nothing. Cormac simply looked at her, a little frown between his brows, his mouth no more than a hardened line. He gave a little jerk of his head, clearly impatient for her to get out of the car so he could move on.

'Bye,' she finally said, and slipped out into the rain.

The driver brought her bags to the door and she was still fumbling with her keys when the car pulled away. Cormac hadn't even bothered to wait to see her inside.

She knew as soon as she stepped across the threshold that Dani was home. There was a spill of clothes in the hall, a pile of dirty dishes in the sink.

Lizzie smiled at the sight. Even though Dani's return brought a whole host of problems, she was glad not to be alone, even if just for a little while. Even if the aching loneliness that had opened up inside her like a wound was still there, raw, weeping, unhealed.

Sleep was still far away, so she put the kettle on and went to change into more comfortable clothes.

A glance at the contents of her luggage had her pushing the suitcase into the corner of the room. She didn't want those clothes, those reminders of a life she was never going to live.

She peeped in on Dani, saw her huddled form in the bed. Dani stirred at the creak of the door, sat up and blinked sleep out of her eyes.

'Lizzie…'

'Oh, Dani.' A lump settled in Lizzie's throat and she swallowed past it as she went to embrace her sister. 'I'm so glad to see you.'

'I'm glad to see you, too.' Sleepily Dani put her arms around Lizzie, laid her head on Lizzie's shoulder.

'I'm sorry I didn't come home earlier,' Lizzie whispered. 'It was…complicated.'

Dani gave her a glimmer of a smile. 'I thought I heard a man in the background when I was talking to you.'

Lizzie, to her dismay, flushed, and Dani laughed. 'I thought it was business!'

'It was,' Lizzie returned grimly. 'It absolutely was.'

The kettle began to sing shrilly and Lizzie rose from the bed. 'Go back to sleep. We'll talk in the morning.'

Alone at the kitchen table, her hands cradled around a mug, she found Cormac's words coming back to her.

Your lonely, loveless little life.

The house was quiet, dark. Dank. Even with Dani upstairs, Lizzie was conscious of the empty spaces—spaces in her home, her heart, her life.

Spaces that she'd been too busy to fill, too determined to be everything to Dani when there was no one to be *anything* to her.

Spaces.

She wanted them filled—somehow, some way.

Not Cormac.

How? Who?

She put her mug down and, as tiredness crashed over her once more, she lay her head on her arms.

The office seemed very quiet without Cormac when Lizzie went in the next day. It was still raining, cold and grey, and her hair was plastered against her face as she arrived and set about shedding her wet things.

There were three pages of detailed instructions and dictations from Cormac, and Lizzie read the strong, slanting handwriting with a pang.

She'd just settled down with her coffee and the first letter to type when one of the assistants from the floor below stopped by her desk.

'There's a rumour going around that you went to the Caribbean with Mr Douglas!' she said, leaning over Lizzie's desk as if for a cosy chat. 'Is it true?'

'Yes,' Lizzie admitted cautiously. 'Mr Douglas was bidding for a commission in Sint Rimbert, and he needed some support staff.'

The assistant, Lisa, nodded enviously. 'What's he like, then? Off the job?'

'We weren't off the job,' Lizzie replied. 'So he was really the same as always.' It came out sounding like a rebuff, and Lisa slouched off, disappointed and annoyed.

Lizzie sighed. How many more rumours was she going to have to stop? How many memories was she going to have to unwillingly relive? And what if news of their sham marriage reached Edinburgh ears?

The architecture world was small—Geoffrey Stears would be putting the news about, and then what?

Either Cormac's deception would be exposed, or she would be roped in to playing wife again. Neither option was remotely appealing.

Everyone knew. Cormac's smile grew strained as he accepted congratulations, commiserations and frank disbelief from colleagues and employees alike.

Geoffrey Stears had done the most damaging thing he could think of—he'd told everyone that Cormac Douglas was married.

Cormac had spent a torturous two days in London, trying to seal the deal with Hassell while everyone in the architecture world came sniffing round for gossip. Confirmation.

Now, on the train back to Edinburgh—to his lovely bride—Cormac knew it would be much more difficult to end his sham marriage without eyebrows raised, questions asked.

Commissions lost.

Damn Geoffrey. Damn Lizzie, for making this all so difficult. For caring.

For falling in love with him.

His mouth twisted. She might have deceived herself that she cared, that he'd cared, but he knew the truth.

She didn't love him because there was nothing to love.

She'd been right—he didn't have anything beneath the hard face he showed the world. He was empty. He'd always been empty, from the moment his mother had left him on a doorstep and walked away for ever.

Or before that, perhaps, when he'd wandered the Edinburgh slums, begging for change because his mum had told him to.

He laughed. If Lizzie knew just how far he'd descended into the depths of hell she wouldn't have deceived herself for a minute. She would have looked at him with hatred, not hope.

Perhaps it would have been better that way.

It didn't matter now; she hated him anyway.

She hated him, and he needed more from her. Now that Stears had spread the news about his marriage, Cormac knew people would be looking to him to confirm it. To show everyone that he was a reformed, loving husband.

The charade would begin once more.

Tonight.

Lizzie's mouth dropped open in surprise when Cormac walked through the door her second afternoon back at work.

'I thought you'd be gone for weeks…' she began.

'Change of plan,' Cormac replied tersely. 'Stears is back in London and letting everyone know we're married.'

Lizzie shrugged. 'You suspected he'd do as much, didn't you?'

'I didn't think he'd be quite so thorough,' Cormac replied grimly. 'If he hadn't been there, no one need ever have known. Hassell doesn't have any links to England—it would never have come out.' He raked a hand through his hair. 'We're going to need to do some damage control.'

'Damage control?' Lizzie repeated, raising her eyebrows. She was amazed at how empty and unemotional she felt. Here was Cormac, bristling with energy and vitality, completely unrepentant about how he'd used her—in fact, planning to use her some more.

And she just couldn't care.

'There's a dinner tonight,' Cormac explained. 'A retired architect, Edward Soames, is getting some award. I wasn't planning to go, but now…'

'Now,' Lizzie guessed, 'it's a perfect opportunity to show off your new wife? Make it look real?'

'Something like that,' Cormac admitted shortly.

Lizzie glanced up, waiting for his request. His command.

'I need you to go,' Cormac said, 'with me.'

She raised her eyebrows. 'You *need* me to go?' she repeated thoughtfully. and Cormac's gaze narrowed.

'You'll come with me, Lizzie,' he informed her curtly. 'We both have too much to lose.'

'Right now I don't feel like I have anything to lose,' Lizzie replied. She returned her gaze to the computer screen, although the letters blurred and danced before her eyes. 'I feel like I've already lost it all.'

Cormac exhaled impatiently. 'If I'd had any idea how melodramatic and heartbroken you'd become, I'd never have asked you to Sint Rimbert.'

'I wish you hadn't,' Lizzie returned with just as much force. Their eyes met and for a brief moment that sentiment seemed to bind them together…in, Lizzie realised bleakly, a hostile web of lies.

She wore the silver dress. It was the only remotely appropriate thing she had in her wardrobe. She gazed expressionlessly at her reflection in her bedroom mirror, wondered if she would ever feel again. If the numbness would go away.

If she wanted it to.

'Wow, you look fantastic, Lizzie.' Dani stood in the doorway, clearly dressed to go out herself, although, Lizzie suspected, to an entirely different sort of venue.

She gave a pale smile. 'Thanks.' It had been good having Dani home, although a bit tense. She knew she needed to give her sister time to reorganise her dreams, just as Lizzie felt she ought to do herself. And she needed the time, too. Time to heal... time to feel.

Yet the questions about the future—both of theirs—were still there, unanswered. Waiting to be solved.

'Are you going out with that man—the one from the weekend?' Dani asked.

Lizzie sighed. 'My boss. Yes. But it's just work. There's nothing between us.'

'You sure about that?' Dani teased, and Lizzie smiled tightly.

'Yes. Absolutely.'

The doorbell rang. Cormac had insisted on picking her up at her home so they would show up at the dinner together. A happy couple.

'Is that him?' Dani asked.

'Yes, but...'

Before Lizzie could say another word, Dani was flying down the stairs.

'Hello, you must be Dani.' She heard Cormac's voice, low and melodious, drift up the stairs. She heard Dani's girlish giggle in response and cringed.

'I'm ready, Cormac.' She put on her matching silver wrap, met his amused gaze with a hard one of her own. She didn't want him here, touching her life, affecting Dani. She didn't want him.

'Brilliant.' He helped her with her wrap, his fingers briefly caressing her bare shoulders. 'You look stunning, Lizzie,' he murmured. She flushed and said nothing. He turned to Dani. 'Nice to meet you, Dani.'

He didn't speak again until they were in his car, a sleek sports model. 'What's wrong?'

'What's wrong?' Lizzie gave a short laugh of disbelief. 'What's wrong? What *isn't* wrong?' She leaned her head back against the seat.

'It will be over soon,' Cormac said after a moment, his voice flat, and Lizzie nodded. That was the only hope she had to cling to.

The dinner was at the Balmoral, Edinburgh's luxury hotel right on Princes Street.

Cormac pulled the car up to the kerb, the hotel's famous clock tower gleaming above them.

A valet opened the door and Lizzie stepped out, feeling grown-up and glamorous. Cormac came to her side, his arm around her waist, drawing her to him.

'Cormac! How lovely to see you.' The bored drawl could only belong to one man—Geoffrey.

'Came all the way from London for this?' Cormac said with a cynical smile, and Geoffrey offered a saccharine smile back.

'Wouldn't miss it for the world.'

He'd come to spy on them, Lizzie knew. To catch them out.

'Feeling well, Elizabeth?' he practically purred. 'You look a bit peaky.'

'Jet lag,' she said shortly. 'It's cold out here—Cormac, will you take me inside?'

'Of course.' They walked through the double doors, into a wide foyer with a blazing fire, marble floors and a chandelier sparkling high above them.

Guests in evening dress circulated, murmuring and chatting, and Lizzie was conscious of the sudden hush and speculative looks as Cormac made an entrance with her on his arm.

His wife.

The evening passed with agonizing slowness. The cocktail hour was an endless parade of introductions, speculative looks and sly remarks, no one quite able to believe that Cormac Douglas had married.

It made Lizzie sad somehow, to think that his reputation was so known—so fixed—that no one could believe he would love a woman. That a woman would love him.

Cormac was as charming as always, smiling and relaxed, but

there were shadows in his eyes. Shadows she'd never seen before. She wondered—or was it hoped?—that the pretence was wearing thin for him, too.

That maybe he didn't want to pretend any more. Maybe he wanted to be real. Genuine, even if it was genuine indifference, would be better than the pretence of affection. Of love.

Somehow she got through the dinner, the speeches, smiling and clapping and nodding even though she was weary and worried and ready to go home.

'I'm going to the ladies',' she whispered to Cormac during an interval between speeches, and slipped out of the opulent banquet room.

The hall was richly carpeted, her footsteps muffled, and as she wandered looking for the loo she wasn't aware that someone was behind her until she heard a steely, silky voice enquire, 'Going somewhere, Lizzie?'

She spun around. Geoffrey stood there, smiling unpleasantly.

Her heart bumped uncomfortably but she still managed a cool smile. 'Actually, I'm looking for the ladies'.'

'You look rather flushed. I thought perhaps it was all getting a bit too much for you.'

'A bit too boring,' Lizzie corrected coldly. 'Now, if you'll excuse me…' She turned away, but Geoffrey grabbed her arm and pulled her back to face him.

His face was twisted with fury into a perverse mask. 'Don't think you'll get away with this,' he snarled. 'I know Cormac has paid you—whether in services or money I can only guess—to pretend to be his wife. Hassell may be fooled, but I'm not!'

His fingers dug into her wrist and Lizzie felt a frisson of fear. 'Let me go,' she commanded in a voice that didn't waver nearly as much as her insides did.

Geoffrey shook his head. 'You don't even know what kind of man he is, do you? People may respect him for his damned designs, but nobody likes him. Nobody wants him here.'

'You obviously don't,' Lizzie observed. She pulled her arm from his now slick grasp. 'I have no idea why you hate him so much—'

'Do you know what he is?' Geoffrey demanded. His throat worked convulsively and his eyes were feverish.

'I know he won a commission you wanted—'

'He came from the street!' There was a strange note of triumph in Geoffrey's hoarse, hostile voice. 'His mother was a drug addict—she used to make him beg for spare change to support her habit.'

Lizzie stared at him. 'How do you know this?'

'I made it my business to find out,' Geoffrey snarled. 'Cormac tries to cover up his beginnings, tries to pass himself off as one of us, but he's not. He never will be. He didn't even go to school properly—he took night classes at a third-rate university. No one would take him on as an associate, he had no credentials. He had to take every piss-poor commission that nobody wanted.' Geoffrey laughed; it was an ugly sound. 'He was designing petrol stations for pennies!'

'Was he?' Lizzie lifted her chin. 'Well, he obviously succeeded—he's not designing petrol stations any more.'

Geoffrey thrust his face near hers. 'He's only succeeded because he intimidates, blackmails or bribes everyone he meets! He doesn't deserve it—he doesn't deserve anything! You have no idea what kind of man he really is—'

'No—' Lizzie cut him off with quiet coolness '—I realise I don't.'

She turned away; Geoffrey grabbed her arm again.

'Get your hands off my wife.'

Lizzie had never been so relieved to hear Cormac's cold, steely voice.

Geoffrey cringed before he shrugged with drunken belligerence. 'I've just been telling your so-called wife a few details about—'

'Yes—' Cormac cut him off '—I heard.' He turned to Lizzie, his face blank, his voice flat. 'The speeches have ended. We can go.'

Lizzie nodded, strangely affected by—and afraid of—the alarming neutrality of both his face and words. How much had he heard? And was it true?

Outside, a needling rain was falling and the pavement was

slick. Lizzie stumbled once in her heels and Cormac reached for her elbow to steady her, his fingers closing around her arm as a matter of indifferent instinct, his face averted.

She sneaked a peep at his profile—he looked preoccupied, his gaze shuttered and distant, his mouth a thin, hard line.

They didn't speak in the car and the only sound was the rain hitting the windows and the methodical swish of the windscreen wipers.

Lizzie's mind spun with the implications of Geoffrey's vitriolic revelations. Was his attitude shared by other architects? Did they actually resent Cormac's success—masked as disgust at where he came from?

And had Cormac really come from such a place? The idea was surprising, shocking. She'd had no idea he'd had to fight so hard to establish himself as an architect. The only press she'd read about him was either to do with his women or his designs. Never his past.

She wondered who he'd paid to keep such stories out of the press. She could hardly blame him; he was not a man to invite either pity or contempt.

'Hassell's ringing me tomorrow,' he said abruptly. 'I believe he'll officially offer me the commission.'

Lizzie swallowed. 'And then…?'

He smiled sardonically, his eyes still on the road. 'And then we're done, Chandler. I have no need of you any more.'

Lizzie blinked. She felt sad, and she didn't even know why, but she *felt*. Her throat ached as she said quietly, 'Good.'

Cormac nodded, silent, and Lizzie forced herself to continue. 'When this is over, I'm going to start looking for another job—perhaps even in a different city.' She hadn't realised she'd harboured such ambitions until she'd spoken them, but now she knew it was what she needed. Escape. Respite. Distance.

Cormac gave a tiny shrug. 'Fine.'

And somehow his complete indifference to her possible absence from his life hurt. It cracked the numb shell that had guarded her heart and made her realise how much she'd started to care.

It hurt far more than it should because, really, there was no reason to think that Cormac cared about her—could ever care. No reason at all.

Cormac pulled up to the kerb in front of her house, its windows lifeless and dark. He jerked his head in a motion of farewell.

Lizzie slid out of the car without a word. The best thing for her, she knew, would be to never see Cormac again. To leave him far behind.

As soon as possible.

The car was still there, the headlights burning into the foggy darkness, as she let herself into the house.

'Cormac, it's Jan.'

Cormac heard the tension and unhappiness in the older man's voice and leaned back in his chair, keeping his own voice light and easy.

'Jan, good to hear from you. I have my preliminary plans for the Sint Rimbert resort right here on my desk.'

'Yes, well…' Jan sighed '…we need to talk about that.'

'Oh?' Cormac's hand curled more tightly around the telephone.

'Cormac, I've heard some things—some disturbing things.'

'The architecture world is a club, Jan, a clique. There's always nasty gossip.'

'I'd like to believe it's just gossip,' Jan admitted.

'Tell me what it is, then,' Cormac said, but he knew. Of course he knew.

'Someone has told me that you and Lizzie aren't actually married. That you hired her to pretend to be your wife!' Jan's voice rang with indignation, as if he expected Cormac to be as outraged as he was…or hoped as much.

'That's ridiculous,' Cormac said calmly.

'Is it? Because, frankly, Cormac, I've begun to wonder. I knew your reputation before I agreed to let you come on this weekend. You're a playboy, a…'

'My reputation in the tabloids,' Cormac corrected. 'Which is exaggerated, and in the past.'

'Maybe so, but I have to tell you that you weren't my first choice for the commission, because of that reputation. Your designs changed my mind, but you have to understand that this resort is important to us, Cormac.' Jan's voice turned almost pleading. 'My own sons have left Sint Rimbert, have pursued lives much like yours in London and New York. When you told me you'd married—you sounded so happy, so different from what I'd expected—I was eager to believe. Perhaps too eager.'

Cormac was silent. He wasn't sure what to say, how to play Jan in this mood.

'Well?' the older man demanded. 'What do you have to say for yourself?'

'I don't know, Jan.' Cormac made himself sound regretful. 'If you're going to believe such jealous rumours, how can I convince you of my sincerity, or the truth of my marriage? Send you my marriage certificate?' He injected a faint note of disapproval in to his voice.

Jan went on hastily, 'No, nothing like that. But perhaps you could have me to dinner—you and Lizzie. I'm coming to London tomorrow, to visit my son, and I can easily nip up to Edinburgh the day after.'

Cormac was silent, digesting this information, his mind racing with possibilities. Problems. 'That would be lovely,' he finally said. 'Lizzie will be thrilled.'

A few minutes later he hung up the phone and stared broodingly at the darkening sky. He had no illusions that Lizzie would agree to a final charade. He'd pushed her as far as she would go. Money, threats, seduction. A simple *please* wouldn't work now.

She was weary enough, disillusioned enough to quietly—or perhaps not so quietly—confess everything to Jan, and Jan, already knowing Cormac's reputation, would be quick to believe the worst. Of him.

As everyone always was. Always had been.

So what could he do? He glanced down at the sketchbook on his desk, the strong pencil lines he'd drawn with his own hand, his own heart.

Cormac frowned and drummed his fingers, a restless energy surging through him, filling him with dissatisfaction.

He knew what he had to do.

There was, he realised, no real choice to make. His choices

had been made for him a long time ago, by other people who had been intent on using him, on making him the man he was—one who would never be used.

And yet...

No. The commission mattered, that was all. Nothing else could. Nothing else would.

He knew what kind of man he was. Even Lizzie knew it now.

And yet...

He sat there for a long time, motionless and brooding, as dusk fell over the city, until all was covered in darkness.

CHAPTER TWELVE

'I WANT you to come with me.'

Lizzie jerked around in surprise, her hands still on the buttons of her coat.

'What?' Her eyes narrowed. 'Where?' And why? was more to the point, but she simply pressed her lips together and waited.

'I want you to come with me,' Cormac replied in a gruff tone, 'to a building site in the Highlands. Now, so don't bother taking your coat off.'

'You've never taken me to a building site before,' Lizzie protested, fruitlessly, she knew, because Cormac was still her boss.

'Now I am.' He gave her the glimmer of a smile. 'Don't look so suspicious.'

'Cormac, if there's one thing I've learned, it's to be suspicious of you,' she replied flatly. 'A valuable lesson.'

'Well, there's nothing to be suspicious of now,' he returned, his voice light. 'I have to check on the golf resort I designed. They've started building and have run into budget problems. I need you to take notes at a meeting with the developers in Inverness, and then come with me to the building site in Strathglass.'

She stared at him, her hands on her hips. 'That's all?'

He paused. 'That's all.'

It wasn't until they were in his car that he remembered to add, 'We need to stop by your house and pick up a few things. We'll be staying the night.'

Lizzie stiffened and jerked around. 'You neglected to mention that little detail.'

'Did I?' He raised his eyebrows, unconcerned. 'Well, it's not that important, is it? Strathglass is quite a drive and I don't know how long the meeting will take. You might have expected we'd be staying the night.'

'And what if I have plans? My sister—'

'Cancel them.'

Her hands bunched into fists in her lap. 'You don't really need me at this meeting, do you?'

His hands flexed on the steering wheel. 'Maybe not,' he admitted.

Lizzie shook her head. She was so tired of guessing, fearing, suspecting. 'Why are you taking me, then?' she asked tiredly.

Cormac was silent for a long moment. 'I just am,' he said, his tone final and a little bleak. Lizzie glanced at him, wondering… and wishing she wasn't.

They drove silently to her house and Cormac pulled the car up to the kerb. 'Be quick.'

'What kind of things do I need?'

'Jeans, jumpers, boots. It's cold, wet and rural.' He gave her another smile, one that made her heart beat just a little too fast. 'Sounds glamorous, doesn't it?'

'Oh, very,' she replied, and climbed out of the car. It only took her a few minutes to stuff some clothes in a holdall, leave a message for Dani and lock up.

Yet when she climbed back into the car, Cormac was scowling once more.

'You're selling your house?' He pointed to the For Sale sign staked outside.

'Yes.' She and Dani had met the estate agent yesterday afternoon. The agent had been thrilled at such a property finally coming on the market and had assured them it would sell quickly.

Then Lizzie would be able to move on. Move away. It was the best thing, the healthiest thing, the *right* thing to do. Even if it hurt. Especially if it hurt.

'I decided to take your advice,' she added with a blaze of determination, 'and get on with my life. I'm going to move to a flat, maybe even take a course.' They were reckless, unformed plans, yet they felt like armour. Weapons. *See, I'm going to manage just fine without you.*

Weapons which bounced off Cormac's indifferent soul. He pressed his lips together and shrugged. 'Fine. Just wait a few days.'

'I thought Hassell was ringing you today, anyway,' Lizzie said.

'Today, tomorrow, whenever.' Cormac spoke in a tone of such blatant unconcern that Lizzie narrowed her eyes.

'Has something changed?' she asked, and he shook his head. 'No.'

'Look at me, then.'

'I'm driving,' he reminded her, coolly amused, and Lizzie sat back in her seat.

A few more days and she'd be gone. Free. From Cormac. The thought was a lifeline, and yet it felt like a deadweight.

They left the dreary city streets for the motorway north, the River Forth winding in a slate grey ribbon through the brown hills.

They drove in silence for several hours. Lizzie stared out of the window as the fields and hills gave way to deep glens— craggy, austere and beautiful.

Cormac seemed preoccupied, frowning, sometimes glancing at her as if he resented her presence. Yet he'd been the one to ask her along. Lizzie couldn't understand it. Didn't want to. She knew the answer would only irritate her and probably hurt her in ways she didn't want to acknowledge.

They drove first to Inverness to meet the developers. As she and Cormac took their seats in a conference room the architectural blueprints were spread out on the table.

The next hour was spent discussing changes the developers wanted made, mainly to cut costs.

Lizzie listened and made notes, glad that she was at least doing something useful. She also found herself listening to Cormac, watching the way he gestured with his hands, long-fingered with square nails, palms brown and hardened from work. She listened to his voice, steady but with an impassioned undercurrent that showed he cared about this resort, this vision.

More than anything else.

She saw the blaze of determination in his eyes, the way it lit his face, tensed his body, filled him with a pulsing excitement and energy.

In a way a person—a woman—*she*—never would. Never could.

When they finally adjourned, everyone seemed satisfied. Cormac had managed to find ways to cut costs and maintain the integrity of his design. They shook hands, laughing and smiling, and Cormac left the building with a firm, light step.

'Where to now?' Lizzie asked when they returned to the car.

'I need to check on the building site and then we can have some dinner.'

After half an hour in the car Cormac pulled into a building site on the side of a deep loch, no more than a concrete foundation on a cleared patch of earth.

Lizzie followed him, picking her away across the hard, packed dirt. A freezing wind blew from the loch and stung her face. She now understood what Cormac had meant by cold, wet and rural.

The foreman shook hands with Cormac and began to walk off with him. Lizzie stood there uncertainly until Cormac turned back and held out his hand.

'You can come, too.' He paused. 'I want you to see it.'

'You do?' Lizzie couldn't keep the blatant surprise—and even disbelief—out of her voice.

'Yes,' Cormac said, a bite of impatience to his voice now, and Lizzie shrugged.

'All right.' She started to pick her away across the muddy concrete, but then Cormac grasped her elbow to steady her, and his hand slid into hers, clasped it with a strength that told her he wouldn't let her go.

And she didn't want him to.

No, no, no. This was not happening again. She was not falling for him again, wanting him again.

Getting hurt again.

She'd learned that lesson. So well.

She was leaving. She had plans, dreams of a life without Cormac, a life that was *safe*.

Yet she didn't even try to slip her hand from his. She didn't even want to.

Apparently she hadn't learned that lesson quite well enough.

For the next hour Lizzie stood by Cormac's side, her hand clasped with his, listening as he went over developments in the project's progress with the foreman.

Occasionally he glanced at her, quick, searching glances that still shook her to the bone.

What was going on? She knew he must have some aim in mind, some image he was trying to project. Surely he didn't think he could fool her again…make her fall for him again.

Yet even now she was tempted, craving the contact, the slide of his hand and the way his gaze darted towards her, as if they shared something more than a deception.

Even now, when she knew it had to be fake, when everything about him was calculated.

It's not real. It's never real.

When they finally returned to the car, it was late afternoon and the sun was low in a sky that had cleared to a pale, fragile blue, the clouds like smoke against the horizon.

'Where to now?' Lizzie asked as Cormac drove away from the site.

'There's an inn near here, in Strathairn. I made us a reservation.' He spoke tonelessly, then gave himself a little shake and slid her a smiling glance. 'How does a roaring fire, a hot toddy and a juicy steak sound?'

'Lovely,' Lizzie said, her voice a bit flat, unable to hide her frown. Something didn't feel right. When had she and Cormac ever shared an honest conversation, an *easy* one? How on earth could they chat over a meal as if they were lovers? Or even friends?

From the way Cormac gazed broodingly at the darkened road, even he recognised the impossibility of such a situation. The falseness.

'Cormac…'

'What?' He was still staring at the road, his profile harsh.

'Why did you bring me here? I wasn't really needed.' Lizzie swallowed. 'So you must have had some reason… You didn't introduce me as your wife, so what's going on?'

'Nothing.' He spoke flatly, but Lizzie wouldn't be put off. Not this time.

'Don't tell me you just wanted my company.'

He shot her a quick, amused glance. 'Is that so hard to believe? I've enjoyed your *company* before.'

She flushed painfully. 'Perhaps, but that's not going to happen again.'

'Why not?'

'Don't play games with me!' she cried fiercely. 'I've told you, I've had enough. You've used me and used me again and I'm *sick* of it!' The words came out, savage and sincere. She slapped her hand against the window in frustration. 'Don't you get tired of using people? Of being such a…'

'Such a what?' he asked softly, and Lizzie didn't heed the warning in those whispered words.

'Such a bastard,' she finished flatly. 'And I'm not talking about your parents, Cormac, I'm talking about your soul. Your heart…if you even have one. Don't you *ever* care about hurting people?' The question was asked in raw, aching honesty. She wanted to know. She had to know.

Cormac was silent for a long moment, his fingers curled tightly around the steering wheel. 'Sometimes,' he said quietly, and Lizzie sagged against the seat.

Sometimes. *When?*

She stared blindly out of the window as the sun sank even lower in the sky, clouds streaming across the glens like golden ribbons.

She hated that even now she wondered what kind of man he really was. Even when she knew, when he'd used her, discarded her and used her yet again, she still hoped.

Hoped what?

What could there possibly be left to hope for?

Twilight was stealing softly over the hills, cloaking them in purple, when Cormac drove into the village.

It was an unassuming place, a few stone cottages and terraced houses around a green that was riddled with muddy puddles.

Cormac drove through the village, then turned on to the high street, quaint and narrow, the old sloped buildings leaning into the road.

Lizzie saw the sign for the inn, on a timbered building that looked every bit as quaint and cosy as she could have hoped.

Cormac began to slow down, switching on the indicator. He began to turn the wheel, then with a hard jerk straightened the car and drove past the inn.

Lizzie glanced at him, surprised, wary. His jaw was clenched tight, his gaze shadowed, shuttered.

'Cormac…?'

'I have one more building to check on.'

'You do?' Lizzie nibbled her lip uncertainly. 'But I thought…'

'I've changed my mind.' There was a finality to his tone, a darkness that sent shivers racing down her back and arms, made her whole body want to tremble.

She watched and waited as Cormac turned down a darkened track that ended at a large stone house nestled in a copse of birch trees.

'It's a house,' she said in surprise. 'And you couldn't have designed it.' The house was three storeys, with gabled windows and a glass-covered front porch. It had to be a hundred years old.

'You're right there,' Cormac agreed as they both got out of the car. 'I'm not that old.'

'How old *are* you?' Lizzie asked impulsively.

'How old do you think I am?'

'Pushing forty, I suppose,' she said with studied nonchalance, and he let out a sharp bark of laughter.

'Thirty-five, actually. And I already know you're twenty-eight.'

Twenty-eight and a virgin. 'From my CV. Yes. Are we going inside?'

The wind was cold and the night was falling fast, turning the world to darkness around them.

'Yes.' He took some keys from his pocket. 'We are.'

The gravel crunched under their feet as they walked across

the drive and Cormac unlocked the door to the porch, ushering Lizzie inside.

He flipped on the lights and Lizzie saw immediately why this house was one of his projects. The inside had been completely renovated, transformed into a light, airy space.

'I'll turn the heating on,' Cormac said as Lizzie walked slowly through the rooms.

It was clearly a house meant for a family. There was a large, bright kitchen with windows overlooking the glen, now no more than shapes and mounds in the darkness. The wide, pine table, the lounge with its squashy settees and tables spoke of no pretence of elegance, just easy comfort.

'Let me show you the upstairs,' Cormac said, and led her up the steep, twisting stairs to the bedrooms.

There were four bedrooms: a nursery, two children's rooms and a master bedroom, each decorated as if waiting for a family to live and love there.

Lizzie stood in the middle of the master bedroom, which was decorated simply in beige and cream, a bed with an oak headboard the main centrepiece. Wide windows opened on to a view to the hills. There was an old fireplace, a basket of coal waiting neatly next to it.

'Whose house is this?' she asked. 'And why don't they live here?' The house was decorated, finished, ready for the perfect family to move in. She could almost hear the echo of their laughter in the rooms, wanted it for herself. 'Your work is done.'

Cormac had been watching her from the doorway, but now he moved into the room. His face was drawn, his eyes remote, hands shoved deep in his trouser pockets. He crossed the wide pine planks of the floor and propped one shoulder against the window frame, staring out into the inky darkness.

'Actually, it's mine.'

Lizzie felt a jolt, a bump, as if she'd been coasting along and had come to a sudden stop. 'Yours? But…'

'Oh, I don't use it. I hardly ever come here.' He flashed her a quick, mirthless smile before turning back to the window and the darkness. 'I just like to have it.'

'It's a family house,' Lizzie said, and Cormac understood what she meant.

'And I'm not a family man. Yes, I know. Stupid, isn't it, to hold on to it? I was planning to sell it. Perhaps I should.'

'Don't.' It came out inadvertently, yet Lizzie knew she meant it. Somehow she felt that this house was a part of Cormac, a glimpse into his soul, his humanity. He couldn't give that up. She wouldn't let him.

'I saw it when I first began designing the golf resort last year,' he explained. 'It was a wreck, but I thought I'd fix it up—a private project—and sell it on. Then I decided to keep it for myself.' He paused. 'I always wanted a house like this as a child.'

'Did you?' Lizzie whispered. She reached out and wrapped a hand around the bedpost. She felt the need to steady herself, to anchor herself in this swirling sea of memories and shadows. 'You never had a home like this, I suppose,' she continued quietly.

'No,' he agreed, then gave a little laugh. 'No.'

The silence stretched between them, tense and dark and strange. Cormac continued to gaze out of the window into the darkness, as if he could see something. His head was averted, and moonlight washed over the strong line of his jaw.

'I shouldn't have brought you here,' he said tonelessly.

Lizzie whispered, 'Why not?'

He gave an imperceptible shake of his head, lost in his thoughts. 'I don't know why I did.'

'Why don't you live here?' Lizzie asked. 'You could commute to the city.'

He shook his head again. 'Why *should* I live here?'

'If you married…had children…' It sounded—and seemed—impossible.

Cormac laughed, a dry, humourless sound. 'Oh, Lizzie. You know that's never going to happen. I'm not that kind of man.'

'You could become that kind of man.'

'No.' He spoke with a terrible finality that echoed through the room, the house, her heart.

'Just because you never had a family of your own…' Lizzie began hesitantly, because she'd never spoken about Cormac's past, didn't know if he'd want her to.

'You're referring, of course, to dear Geoffrey.' Cormac turned to her with a faint smile, an eyebrow raised. 'He told you all my sordid secrets.'

Lizzie shrugged helplessly, unsure of what to say.

'I suppose he shocked you, but every word is true. My mother was a heroin addict. She left when I was seven.'

Lizzie swallowed. 'What happened then?'

'I went into care. A care home, actually. On Cowgate.'

'The office,' Lizzie realised. He'd redeemed his past in that way, at least.

'Yes.'

'Were you happy there?' Lizzie asked. She felt as if she were picking her way across a minefield of memories. She had no idea which ones would explode.

'Happy…' Cormac repeated musingly. 'It was run by a drunk and the children were either bullied or bullies themselves. You learned quickly.'

'Which one were you?' Lizzie whispered, and he flashed her a quick, cold smile.

'Can you guess?'

Lizzie nodded, her throat tight. He had been seven years old, malnourished, uncared for, afraid. Suddenly she was beginning to understand…understand so much. And it hurt.

She hurt again. She *felt* again. A rush of pain and sorrow for the man before her, the man shaped by brutality and indifference, and yet who had risen above it to design buildings of beauty and grace.

That man.

'How long were you in care?' she asked when she felt she could speak in a normal voice.

'Eight years in the home. No one wanted me.' He spoke with such dispassionate calm that she wanted to shake him, touch him, hurt him. Make him feel. 'Then I was fostered to a family, the father was a carpenter. He took me on as his apprentice.' He was silent, still staring out of the window, lost in thought.

'Was he a good man?' Lizzie asked.

'Not particularly.' Cormac gave a little laugh. 'No, not particularly.' He lapsed into silence again.

That didn't sound very good, Lizzie thought. She felt as if she were reaching the heart of Cormac's darkness, of his self.

And she didn't know what to do. What questions to ask.

'Did he get you started in architecture?' she finally said.

Cormac was silent for a long, brooding moment. 'I suppose you could say he did,' he replied. 'He taught me many things.' He paused. 'When I was eighteen, I applied to a school of architecture, a decent one. I had no money, of course, but I thought if I showed them my designs I might get a scholarship.' He paused, shrugged. 'I was accepted, the scholarship, the whole works. Only I didn't know. My foster father got to the letter first and destroyed it. Told me I'd been rejected. He wanted me to stay with him, you see. Unpaid apprentice. I was very *useful* to him.' He shook his head again, closed his eyes briefly before snapping them open, gazing out at the world with the hardened expression Lizzie knew so well.

'So you went to night school,' Lizzie whispered. 'Worked your way up.'

'Yes. And aggravated men like Stears, who can't stand to see someone actually earn their success.' He shook his head. 'I don't mind having enemies. I expected it.'

Lizzie nodded slowly. She was beginning to understand about the ghosts in his past, the ghosts that mocked and drove him— the ghosts that had turned his heart to buildings, because they were beautiful and they never let you down.

They never hurt you. They never used you.

As Cormac had been used—again and again.

'It wasn't until years later,' Cormac resumed, his tone eerily conversational, 'when I was celebrating my first commission, that I came across someone from the admissions board who remembered my name. My application. He wondered why I hadn't accepted.'

'Did you confront your foster father?' Lizzie asked in a whisper.

'Yes. He admitted it all. And really, Lizzie, I should have known. I should have known all along that he was using me, because I'd always known the truth. Always.' He paused, and

Lizzie's heart stopped. She knew she didn't want to hear this. Not from Cormac. Not now. Not this.

He turned to her, eyes glittering with icy determination even in the shadowy room. 'The truth is, Lizzie, that people are users. You either use or let yourself be used. You may lie, pretend, cheat or bribe—you may even deceive yourself—but that's what it comes down to. And I understood that. You don't grow up in foster homes without learning what people are really like.'

She shook her head, her throat tight with suppressed emotion. Suppressed need. 'Not everyone is like that, Cormac.'

'No,' he contradicted flatly, 'everyone is. Everyone I've ever known. Everyone. In fact…' he looked at her now with a new bleakness in his eyes, an emptiness that unnerved her, undid her, because it was so unlike him '…I brought you on this trip as part of a ploy. I was going to flatter you, keep you sweet. Seduce you again.'

Her mouth opened soundlessly and he laughed, a sharp echo without any humour at all. 'I know, it was going to be rather difficult. Once bitten, twice shy. I needed to think very carefully how I was going to go about it.'

She stumbled back against the bed, closed her eyes against a tide of nausea and unbearable disappointment. 'How were you, then?' she whispered.

'Oh, I had it planned. It had to be different from last time, I knew that. I was going to admit I was wrong. I was going to be open and honest and so very vulnerable. I was even…' he paused, drew in a ragged breath '…going to tell you that I love you.'

'But you don't.'

He shrugged. 'Jan Hassell is coming to dinner tomorrow night. He's flying to Edinburgh from London to check on us. Stears told him we weren't married, and he suspects the truth.'

Lizzie blinked, tried to take it in. 'So you thought if I believed you loved me, I'd go along with it?'

'Wouldn't you?'

'Yes,' she whispered. 'Yes.' Her throat was raw and aching with the effort of trying not to cry.

'So you see,' Cormac finished flatly, 'we're all users.'

'How am I using you, Cormac?'

'You think you love me. You want to love me, perhaps to fix me, to make your life look better. Feel better. Don't you?'

'I *think* I love you?' Lizzie repeated.

Cormac shrugged. 'Lizzie, if you knew what I was really like—you should by now!—then you'd never love me.'

She swallowed, blinked back tears. 'Wouldn't I?'

'No. You wouldn't.' He paused, then added flatly, 'No one would.'

Or ever had. Lizzie stood up on shaky legs. Her mind spun with the implications of what he'd planned. She would have believed every deceitful word because she was desperate to.

He would have broken her heart.

Yet he hadn't. He'd admitted the truth, painful, hurtful as it was. He'd given her freedom.

Why?

'So why, Cormac,' she asked quietly, 'are you telling me all this now? You're ruining your deal. You might be losing your commission. If you're just intent on using people—on using me—then why?' She held her breath, knowing the answer her heart craved.

Because I care about you. Because I love you.

'Damned if I know.' Cormac laughed; it was a lonely sound. 'Damned if I know why I brought you to this house, or started any of this. We should have gone to the hotel. We'd have eaten oysters and had champagne. I'd be making love to you right now.'

They stood there for a long moment, silent, in the shadows, the only sound the lash of rain on the windowpanes.

Damned if I know. It was, Lizzie realised, as close as Cormac could get to an admission of need. Of love. It wasn't very much at all.

Yet strangely, simply, it was enough. Lizzie knew what she wanted. She knew without question, hesitation or reservation.

She wanted him. The way he was, the way he could be.

'Well,' she said, her voice trembling a little bit, 'you still could.'

Cormac stiffened, then turned around slowly. 'What are you saying?'

Lizzie took another step forward. 'Make love to me, Cormac. I want you. *You.*'

The house shifted and creaked in the wind; a tree branch tapped against the glass.

'You want me,' he repeated slowly. 'But I've just said…'

'I know what you've told me. I understand. I want you. I want you to make love to me. With me.'

Cormac stared at her. His face was open, honest, vulnerable… and he didn't even know it.

'All right,' he whispered, and took a step towards her.

CHAPTER THIRTEEN

CORMAC raised his hands slowly and rested them on her shoulders. They were both tense, waiting, uncertain.

Ready.

He let his hands slide slowly down her arms, the whisper of fabric against his callused skin. His hands touched her own, folded them inside his.

He brought her hands to his lips and Lizzie blinked back tears.

He bent to kiss her, his lips a breath from hers, and then he paused.

Lizzie looked up at him. 'What is it?'

'I don't know how to do this,' he whispered. 'Show me.'

She blinked. 'I think you know very well—'

He shook his head. 'No, I don't. Not like this.'

With a shaky little laugh, Lizzie touched his face, brought his lips to her own. She kissed him softly, inexpertly, yet he moaned and drew her to him, pulled her softness into his own hard planes, and she joined him with a rush of sweet, sweet abandon.

'I want you,' he murmured against her hair, her lips, her throat. 'I want you so much.'

She kissed the salt from the hollow of his throat, felt the pulse beating and jumping there. His hands tangled in her hair and he slowly drew her to the bed.

He laid her on the bed, carefully, as if she might break, and began to unbutton his shirt with fumbling fingers.

He slipped her trousers off, then, with tender hands, began to undress her, his eyes never leaving hers. It felt like the purest form of communication.

He unclasped her bra and slid her panties down her legs with slow reverence.

When she was naked, he finished undressing himself, then lay next to her.

'Show me.'

'I don't know how…' Lizzie began, bemused, a little bit afraid, a lot uncertain.

'I'm not sure I know, either,' Cormac murmured. 'Not like this. Not…for real.' A smile glinted in his eyes as he dipped his head to her breasts. 'But I'm a good learner.'

Lizzie gasped as his tongue caressed her, for instead of the sure, calculated strokes of a clever lover, he was hesitant, as if it were new. As if he were exploring her.

And these caresses filled her with a longing, an unbearable urgency and a poignant understanding that rent her body and soul.

She drove her fingers into his hair, her body arching instinctively. He paused, smiled. 'All right?'

'Yes.' She drew in a ragged breath.

'Now you show me,' he commanded, and Lizzie let out a laugh.

'How…'

Yet somehow she already knew, and she liked the knowledge.

She pushed him on to his back and bent over him, pressing her lips to his chest. His skin was smooth and hard and hot. She let her tongue dart out, exploring the taste of him, salty and sweet.

She moved to his nipple, circled it with her tongue, smiled as she heard his groan.

'Lizzie…you're showing me.' He laughed as his hands tangled in her hair and she daringly moved lower. 'You're showing me.'

She felt his arousal against her throat as she moved lower, and lower still, kissing him until he groaned and drew her up against him.

'My turn again.'

'I like these lessons,' she said breathlessly as he bent to trail kisses across her navel, and then moved lower still. 'Very much…'

She'd never known such sensations existed. Her fingers dropped from his head as she writhed beneath his ministrations, her head thrown back, her mind whirling…

She was teetering on the edge again, on the precipice of complete loss of control, total vulnerability.

'I can't…' she began thickly, and heard him chuckle, the sound a bit ragged.

'Yes,' he said, 'you can.'

'Cormac…'

It was a plea, and it splintered on the night air as she felt herself fall apart, a glorious destruction, as if all the tightly held pieces of herself were scattered. As if she were free.

She cried out again and realised she was weeping, tears wet on her cheeks, yet she didn't care.

'Don't cry.' His voice was hoarse. 'Don't cry, please.'

'No, no.' She cradled his face in her hands, laughing through her tears. 'I'm *happy*. It's so beautiful. You're so beautiful. I want you inside me, Cormac. Come inside me.'

With a smothered groan he did. She was ready for him and barely felt the twinge of pain as he began to move, filling her, consuming her. She moved awkwardly at first, jerking and thrusting in a way that was both unfamiliar and wonderful until she understood the rhythm of it, of their bodies as one.

One.

He looked down at her, his eyes blazing and meeting hers, their gazes locked, and with one hand he reached up to wipe her tears away.

And then it was happening again—the spiralling, the scattering.

The wonderful loss of herself, so that she felt as if she'd been split open to her soul, and it was *all right*.

It was the best thing that had ever happened to her.

She'd thought, in some corner of her mind, that she could heal him.

But she'd been wrong. He'd healed *her*.

* * *

They must have slept, for when Lizzie stirred again she saw that it was late and the room was plunged in darkness.

She glanced at Cormac, his hair tousled, his face relaxed in sleep, and felt something rise up within her, something overwhelming and deep and true.

Love.

She loved him.

Of course it should have been obvious to her; she'd fallen in love with him in Sint Rimbert, perhaps at that first glimpse of the hidden man underneath…the man she believed in.

The man she now knew was there.

That man.

She turned away from him, drew her knees up to her chest. She had no idea what Cormac felt.

She thought of what they'd just shared, the exquisite joy of giving and receiving pleasure, of loving and being loved.

Except—was there really any love on his side? Or was it just another kind of using? Using her body, fulfilling a physical need.

No, it was more than that. It had to be.

Except maybe it didn't.

She closed her eyes. She had no idea what Cormac thought. What he felt. What he expected.

What he was even capable of.

And she was too involved—too in love—too *afraid* to ask.

Cormac stirred, opened his eyes. 'I'm starving.'

'Me, too.'

He glanced at the clock. 'It's after midnight. There'll be nothing open in the village.'

She shrugged. 'I suppose we'll have to wait till morning.'

'Maybe I can find something downstairs…' He stood up, glorious in his nakedness, and went in search of food.

Once he was gone, the cold started to penetrate. Inside her soul, as well as her body.

She wrapped a sheet around herself and moved to the fireplace. Everything was laid out so that it only took a moment before a fire began to burn and crackle.

Cormac came into the room and smiled. 'We have the means of a feast.'

'Oh?' Lizzie raised one eyebrow. 'What did you find?'

'A tin of peaches, another of ham, a carton of UHT milk and some dry biscuits. Emergency provisions I must have left here once.'

She laughed. 'That's quite a feast.'

'Oh, you'd be surprised what I can do with this.' He was still naked, smiling like a schoolboy, and Lizzie laughed as he opened the tin of peaches and ate one sticky slice with his fingers. Then he offered one to her, but instead of handing it to her he raised it to her lips.

Smiling, feeling a little bit naughty, she opened her mouth. The peach was sweet, slippery, and as she saw Cormac watching her Lizzie suddenly felt desire pooling in her middle, rising in a tidal wave of need.

'First we eat,' he said. Still hungry, both for food and for him, she nodded.

They ate there, naked in front of the fire, makeshift sandwiches of ham on biscuits, followed by peaches and milk.

It was the best meal she'd ever had.

Afterwards, he carried her to the bed and they made love again, without speaking, their bodies in new yet natural rhythms, their eyes fastened on each other as if they wanted to share every thought, every emotion.

Every joy.

Later, sated, sleepy, they lay there, Cormac having draped one careless arm over her.

He fell asleep and Lizzie found herself awake, suddenly wide-eyed, alert and aware.

That was when they came—the feelings she'd held back, hidden from herself.

The fear. The shame. The grief.

She'd given away a part of herself—the heart of herself—to a man who might not even want it. Want *her*.

She had no idea what he wanted, only what *she* did. She wanted more than one night. She wanted for ever.

She'd told Cormac she wanted to wait for marriage, or at least for love and respect, but she hadn't waited at all.

Had she?

Hadn't she actually just sold out—sold *herself*—for a bit of affection, one night of pleasure?

Lizzie closed her eyes, bit her lips against the tears and cries that threatened to come.

She had a feeling that Cormac didn't want for ever. It had just been one night for him—one incredible, wonderful, *terrible* night.

Dimly, dully, Lizzie wondered if this night was actually the biggest mistake of her life.

Cormac slid out of the bed. The room was bathed in moonlight, shadowed with darkness. Lizzie slept on, her breathing soft and easy. He padded across the floor, pulled on his trousers and walked downstairs.

All around him the house was silent, still, breathing. His house. Their house.

His mouth twisted in an ironic smile; he was playing pretend. Everything was pretend, unreal. Fake.

He should know. He understood what could be real and what could not, even if Lizzie lived in a land of dreams.

He ran a hand through his hair, closed his eyes briefly. He was so close to having his commission, to having everything he'd ever wanted. Last night had been better than he could have planned, had succeeded past even his own imaginings.

Even if he'd never thought it could happen like that.

It *had*.

Restlessly he prowled around the empty rooms—rooms that had been made ready and waiting for a family. Someone else's family.

Not his, never his, because he'd never had one. Never would.

He wasn't made that way.

Lizzie was bound to be disappointed, and the sooner she realised it, the better. For both of them.

Upstairs a board creaked and with a suppressed oath Cormac started back towards the bedroom. He didn't want Lizzie to wake up and wonder. Not yet.

She still lay curled protectively in sleep, her hair spread out on the pillow. With one finger Cormac stroked its silky softness. In her sleep, she smiled.

Closing his eyes against that smile and what it meant, Cormac slid into bed. His body felt cold next to her own womanly warmth and he knew sleep would be a long time coming.

Cormac was gone when she awoke. She lay there for a moment, still, remembering. The wide bay windows looked out on a deep, impenetrable forest, thick evergreens beneath a low and leaden sky.

She swung her legs over the edge of bed, hunted for the discarded clothes from last night.

She was just pulling on her trousers when Cormac came in to the room.

'I brought your suitcase in.' He placed it by the door. 'You probably want fresh clothes.'

She looked up and their eyes met, the moment silent and heavy.

Cormac's hair was tousled, his feet bare. His eyes swept over her and his expression turned hard. Again. With a faint sardonic smile, he reached down and picked up a discarded sock from the night before.

He tossed it to her and she caught it as a matter of instinct.

'You'll need this,' he said softly. 'For your cold feet.'

He turned and left the room. Lizzie heard him walk down the stairs. She dropped the sock, drew in a shuddering breath.

If he'd smiled, taken her into his arms, given any indication that last night had been real, that it had meant something—she would have told him. Would have told him everything—what last night had meant to her, that she loved him.

Now the words lodged in her throat, in her gut, and she thought she'd never say them. She'd never be given the chance.

Cormac simply thought of this as a one-night stand. Shame scorched her soul at the thought, even though she knew it shouldn't surprise her. He'd never suggested anything else.

Why should he suddenly change? Why should he suddenly want to?

Perhaps this really was all he was capable of…all he knew how to do. Use people.

Use her.

A terrible new thought assailed her. What if last night had been planned? Part of the seduction? *I was going to be open and honest and so very vulnerable. I was even going to tell you that I love you.*

Had his supposed honesty last night been part of a bigger ploy?

Had it *all* been lies, so that now she would act the loving wife to convince Jan…because she believed herself to be loved?

Except she didn't. She wasn't.

Confused and sick at heart, Lizzie sank on to the bed. She didn't know what to think, what to believe.

What to feel, what to say. She was afraid to ask for the truth. She was certainly afraid to know it.

Dressed in jeans and a woolly jumper, she followed the fresh, tantalising scent of brewing coffee downstairs.

Cormac was in the kitchen, frying eggs. 'I went to the village shop while you were getting dressed,' he explained. 'I thought we should have some proper food.'

Lizzie thought of their impromptu feast of peaches and ham and felt a pang of sweet sorrow.

'Yes, thanks, it all looks heavenly.' She spoke awkwardly, as if to a stranger. To her boss.

Cormac threw her a wry, knowing glance before turning back to the frying pan. 'Help yourself to some coffee.'

'I will, thanks.' She poured herself a mug, but her hands were shaking and she spilled some on herself. 'Damn!' She sucked her burned thumb, sudden tears crowding her eyes, stupid tears because the burn didn't hurt.

Everything else did.

Cormac turned around, leaned against the worktop and waited.

'I'm sorry,' Lizzie muttered. 'I'm not used to this.'

'I know that, Chandler. You are—were—a virgin. I can't imagine you understand morning-after protocol.'

'That's what this is? The morning after?' It sounded so sordid.

'What else would it be?'

The start of a relationship, of the rest of our lives. Of nothing.

'No doubt you're an expert,' she answered with a touch of acid. 'So tell me, what should I do?'

Cormac gave her a cool, fleeting smile. 'Unfortunately, I'm not an expert, either. My women don't stay the night, remember?'

She nodded slowly. 'But I did.'

'Yes, you did, and in about half an hour we need to be heading back to Edinburgh.' He raised his eyebrows. 'Remember, Jan is coming to dinner tonight, and we have to play the happy couple.'

He turned back to the eggs, and Lizzie was left clutching her coffee, feeling sick. Playing the happy couple…because that was all it was, all it ever would be.

Playing. Pretend.

That was all he wanted…Hassell believing in this charade.

Perhaps a charade was all he was capable of. Yet surely if last night had been part of a ploy he would still be playing the lover today. Except perhaps he didn't know how.

Perhaps he wasn't *that* good an actor.

It should have brought relief, that at least last night hadn't been planned, a cold, calculated seduction, but it didn't. All it brought was despair.

Whatever last night had meant to Cormac, it had obviously meant much *more* to her.

And that was all that mattered.

So she'd just have to move on, she told herself, torn between hysteria and hopelessness. She'd endure the dinner with Jan tonight and then she would leave. Quit. Escape.

Never see Cormac again.

After a hearty fry-up, of which Lizzie ate very little, they got back into the car for the long drive back to the city.

Lizzie sat there, her mind and heart numb.

After several hours of silence, she finally forced herself to say, 'So after tonight…if Jan offers you the contract…that's it?'

Cormac was silent, his gaze fastened on the road. He flexed his fingers on the steering wheel. 'Yes,' he said after a moment. 'That's it.'

She managed to nod, look unconcerned, when she felt as if every part of her were breaking, scattering into discarded pieces.

'Cormac…did last night…' She swallowed. Her throat was suddenly dusty and dry. 'Did it mean anything? To you?'

He'd pulled to the kerb in front of her house and now he glanced over at her, his fingers tapping the steering wheel. 'What do you think?' he finally asked.

'That's not an answer.'

He shrugged. 'I don't have another one.'

She bit her lip. 'What does that mean? If it was just a one-night stand, you can tell me. I won't be…'

'Hurt? But you're already hurt, Lizzie, I can see it in your eyes.' He shook his head, a savage note entering his voice. 'Didn't I warn you? Didn't I tell you what I was like?'

'Yes,' she whispered. 'You did.'

The air was heavy with tension, with things that had been said and, worse, all the things that hadn't.

He shook his head. 'This wasn't meant to happen.'

'What wasn't? Me? Us?'

'There is no us,' Cormac said in a tone of heavy finality. 'There can't be.'

Tears stung her eyes. 'Last night…'

'Was last night. It was good between us, Lizzie, but that's all it can be. I don't have anything else to give.' He turned to her, a new bleakness in every harsh line and unforgiving angle of his face. 'Lizzie, after tonight I won't ask anything of you. I'll pay you triple what you earn in a year and you can move on…find someone to love. Someone who deserves it. And I'll let you go.'

'But what if…' Lizzie began, her throat raw and aching, only to have Cormac shake his head with firm, relentless decision.

'No. No what ifs. Come to my flat at six.' He averted his head, stared out of the window. 'Jan's coming at seven, but you should get dressed there. It will be more convincing.' He paused, frowning. 'Perhaps you should bring a few things—books, clothes. Photos. Make it look like you actually live there.'

Lizzie stared at him, amazed that he could, even now—especially now—be so cold about the deception. So matter-of-fact.

And expect her to be, too.

'Yes,' she whispered. 'All right.' She lifted her chin. 'And then I will get on with my life. Start it fresh.'

A smile flickered in Cormac's eyes and died.

She opened her mouth and for one second she thought she might shout, shake him, plead even. Do anything to make him admit.

Admit what? That he loved her? Lizzie closed her mouth. The problem was, he didn't. And he'd just told her that, more or less.

He wasn't capable of love. Didn't know how, didn't want to learn.

Last night hadn't been a charade; it had been worse than a charade.

It had been nothing.

The only thing left for her to do was get out of the car, so she did.

'See you tonight,' she choked, and turned towards her house.

Dani wasn't home. Lizzie lay on her bed, trying to rest, to sleep, to blot out the memory of last night and the pain it was now causing her.

The hours passed in gritty, dry-eyed silence, until she realised it was getting late and she began to gather her things. Woodenly she found a few paperbacks, a nightgown, her favourite coffee mug and packed them in a box. They looked like the preposterous props they were.

Cormac's flat was a penthouse in one of the city's luxury high-rises, all chrome and leather, gloss and steel.

Lizzie trailed behind him as he quickly showed her around, wandered the darkened rooms—the rooms of a man who didn't care about his home, who had no home…who never had.

'This is our bedroom.' He spoke flatly.

She followed him to a large room with a view of the glittering skyline, a huge double bed with navy satin sheets, and suddenly she couldn't bear it.

How many women had been here? How many had been shown the door before morning? She was just one more in a long line for whom Cormac had spared a few moments of time, a few moments of pleasure. Nothing more.

How could she ever have thought otherwise?

'You can dress here.'

Lizzie nodded, swallowed. 'Okay.'

Cormac glanced critically around the room. 'And put a few things about—make it look lived in.'

Lizzie swallowed. 'Yes, all right.'

She moved around the room, placing her book by the bed, her nightgown on the chair, her shoes kicked into the corner as if she'd tossed them off without a care.

It felt like setting a stage, and that was exactly what it was.

What would it be like, Lizzie wondered, if it were real? If Cormac really loved her, if she lived here as his wife?

She felt a sharp stab of longing and nearly gasped aloud with the pain of it. She wanted that so much.

So much.

And she wasn't going to have it. It hadn't even crossed Cormac's mind.

She dressed, wearing a plain but elegant sheath in apple green silk, another item from the Cormac Collection.

She put her make-up on, arranged her hair and looked half-heartedly in the mirror. She looked terrible. Washed out, woebe-gone.

And she felt worse.

Cormac knocked once on the door and came in. 'Are you ready?' He glanced around, took in her props. 'I don't think Jan will even come in here, but just in case he checks…well done.'

She choked on a hysterical laugh. 'Thank you.'

He glanced at her, frowned at her tone. 'Lizzie? All I'm asking…'

'Is tonight. I know. Don't worry, I won't blow it. It's too much trouble.'

His mouth tightened. 'I'm glad to hear it.'

Lizzie shook her head, amazed that a man who had been so tender twenty-four hours ago could now look at her as merely a pawn in his plans.

Yet, really, wasn't that all she'd ever been?

The doorbell rang. Cormac left the room and Lizzie leaned her head against the mirror, felt the cold glass against her skin. One more night…a few hours…one final performance and then she was free.

Too bad she didn't *want* to be free.

She heard the low murmur of voices from the lounge and taking a deep breath, turned and opened the door.

'Elizabeth!' Jan turned, the smile on his face becoming a faint frown of concern as he took in her appearance.

Lizzie forced a smile. 'Hello, Jan.'

He kissed her cheek and behind him Lizzie saw Cormac frowning as he watched them. Clearly her performance was not up to par.

'How is Hilda?' Lizzie asked.

'Well, she's well. She's sorry she couldn't be here.'

'So am I.'

Jan looked at her, still frowning slightly, and Lizzie knew he was wondering if she really was Cormac's wife. She was so far from the radiant bride she was meant to be.

'A glass of wine, Jan? I've made reservations for a table at The Tower at half past seven.'

'Very good.' He paused, looking uncomfortable, and Lizzie guessed he probably felt a bit awkward and perhaps even guilty at the way he was checking up on them.

'Would you like a tour of the flat?' Cormac asked.

Jan hesitated. 'Yes…I suppose…' He glanced briefly at the spartan room, clearly a typical bachelor pad.

Lizzie forced a smile. 'I've yet to put my stamp on this place,' she said as Cormac moved through the rooms, showing them to Jan. 'As you can see.'

'We've bought a house, actually,' Cormac interjected. 'Up north. It's a bit of a commute, but it's a wonderful place to raise a family.'

He was talking, of course, about the house in Strathairn. Their house. Using their memories as ammunition, evidence. Polluting her memory of the evening with lies.

Using it…using her.

When would she learn? When would she truly realise that was all Cormac could manage?

Lizzie turned her face away, hardly able to bear it. They returned to the lounge and Cormac poured the wine, gave glasses to both her and Jan.

'A family home is so important,' Jan said, taking a sip.

'Yes, it is.' Cormac's voice was quiet. 'I never had one of my own growing up, so this home is all the more important to me… and I can't imagine anyone but Lizzie in it.'

She spluttered on her wine, made a pretence of choking and put the glass down. 'Sorry…'

Lies. All of it was lies. Lies she wanted to hear, was desperate to believe.

But it had to be lies. Lies he was telling Jan, to get his commission.

It was all about the commission. Still.

Always.

'That's one of the reasons this commission was so important to me,' Cormac continued. 'I didn't realise why courting it was so important to me, but I've come to realise that I've wanted to design something for families—a home of sorts.'

'That is exactly what it should be,' Jan agreed, beaming approval. 'A home. A home for the traveller.' Jan glanced at Lizzie with silent speculation. 'And perhaps you'll have your own home, with children, in time.' He smiled kindly and Lizzie realised he must think she was depressed about not being pregnant yet.

What a joke. Cormac had been careful to use protection last night. Even in the midst of such a mind-shattering event, he'd been in control.

The last thing he wanted was a baby, a family. Yet her hand stole to her stomach anyway, rested on her middle in silent longing.

'Yes, in time,' Cormac agreed, draping an arm around Lizzie's shoulders. 'In the meantime, we're just enjoying being together, aren't we, darling?'

'Oh. Yes.' She couldn't have sounded more unconvincing, yet Lizzie couldn't care. At that moment, she didn't care about Jan, or the commission or Cormac's career. She didn't care about the publicity, the scandal. All she could feel was the breaking apart of her hopes, her dreams, her*self*.

There was a moment of awkward silence and then Cormac cleared his throat. 'Shall we head to the restaurant?'

They took a taxi to Chambers Street, where the exclusive restaurant was located, above the Museum of Scotland. Lizzie stared out of the window while Cormac and Jan talked shop.

As they entered the rooftop restaurant, sleek and elegant, a view of Edinburgh Castle visible from the wide windows, Cormac pulled Lizzie to his side.

'What is wrong with you?' he hissed.

Lizzie pulled away. 'Everything,' she choked, too despairing to dissemble.

'Lizzie…'

She shook her head, unable to speak, and pushed past him into the dining room.

Cormac ordered for her and Lizzie was grateful. She picked at her spinach and Parmesan tartlet, watched and listened as Jan and Cormac made conversation.

'Elizabeth?' Jan questioned as their main courses were removed. 'Are you quite all right, my dear?'

'Lizzie's a bit tired,' Cormac said quickly. 'She's had some trouble with her younger sister and it's taking its toll.'

Jan frowned. 'I'm sorry to hear that.'

'We're sorting it out,' Cormac returned smoothly. 'Together.'

'It's important for a married couple to present a united front,' Jan agreed, clearly approving.

'Absolutely. Lizzie and I have both come to realise that we need to be of one mind. Not just about her sister, but about a lot of things.' He paused, glancing at her and the wooden expression on her face. 'It's so easy to decide things on your own,' he continued quietly, 'but in the end that's a lonely—and loveless— existence. Lizzie's shown me.'

Show me.

And suddenly it was too much. He'd taken everything that was special, that was *sacred*, between them and used it in his appalling charade. Nothing was safe. Nothing was sacred.

Nothing was real.

Lizzie threw down her napkin. 'I'm sorry,' she said in a low voice, 'I need to leave.'

Jan half rose from the table, startled and concerned, but Lizzie shook her head. She could already feel the tears spurting from her eyes.

'No, don't. Neither of you get up.'

'Lizzie—' Cormac reached out a hand, and she backed away.

'No. No, Cormac. I'm sorry. *I'm sorry.*' Her voice broke. 'I can't do this—I can't pretend to feel the things I really feel, even while I'm pretending not to! Does that even make sense? Do you have any idea how hard it is to hear every lie you're spouting and want it to be true? Having to pretend—for Jan—that it *is* true? Every beautiful thing I thought we had last night…you've twisted it, ruined it…' her voice choked despairingly '…*used* it.'

They both stared at her, Jan's face white and appalled, Cormac's hard and blank.

Lizzie continued recklessly, too hurt to care. 'I finally get it. I finally realise that you're using me. It took me long enough, didn't it? I kept hoping that you were better, bigger than that. That I could change you, make you care. But I can't. And I can't pretend to be your wife any more. I can't pretend to love you any more. And the terrible, ironic thing is—I can't because I really do.' Choking back a sob, she pushed past a waiter and headed towards the lift.

She punched buttons blindly, tears obscuring her vision, knowing that she'd created a huge scene, she'd ruined everything.

Except it had already felt ruined before.

She emerged at the bottom of the lift, crying openly, the tears freezing on her cheeks, and began to walk towards home. She didn't care about the cold, the unforgiving wind.

At that moment she didn't care about anything.

Her house was dismal, empty and unloved. There was a note from Dani, scrawled and careless, saying she'd met up with friends.

Dani didn't need her any more, whatever happened with university. Cormac didn't need her.

Nobody needed her. Nobody wanted her.

Lizzie had never before been so conscious of what little she had.

She had nothing.

The future she'd planned for herself—a flat, a course—now seemed so pathetic compared to what she really wanted. What she hoped.

What she could never have.

She put on pyjamas and made a cup of tea, half wondering what Cormac was doing, what he was thinking right now. Had he lost the commission? Would his career be ruined?

She felt a stab of guilt, but it was lost in a haze of misery.

She sat in the kitchen, the tea untouched before her, and stared out at a dark and fathomless sky.

The front door opened and she called out, 'Dani?'

Then Cormac appeared in the kitchen doorway. His hair was mussed, the shoulders of his overcoat damp with rain as they had been the first time he'd come in this house, into her life properly.

And now he would be leaving it.

Their eyes met. Lizzie was conscious of her tear-blotched face, her straggly hair. Cormac's gaze swept over her. Then he took a step inside the room.

'May I sit down?'

She shrugged. He took a chair across from her, his hands in his lap.

'So what happened?' Lizzie finally asked. 'Jan must know… or were you able to spin some incredible story about what I said?' She tried to laugh, didn't quite succeed.

'No,' Cormac answered, 'I wasn't.'

She looked up at him; he gazed back at her steadily.

'Then your career… Is it…?'

'I don't think so. But I've lost the commission.'

She nodded slowly. 'Jan won't tell…?'

'No, he was surprisingly understanding.' Cormac paused. 'I think because I told him that I actually did love you.'

Lizzie jerked her head up. It was too hard to hope. 'More lies,' she said flatly. 'You're really very good at using people, Cormac.'

He nodded. 'Yes, I am. I always have been. I've always thought that's all people were good for.'

Something in his tone, something new and unexpected and honest, made Lizzie ask, 'Don't you still believe that?'

Cormac shook his head. 'No, I don't.'

Lizzie sprang from the table, suddenly restless. She poured her untouched tea down the sink. 'Why isn't Jan giving you the commission, then?' she asked. 'If he was so incredibly understanding.'

'Because I told him to give it to Dan.'

She turned around, her face sharp with suspicion. 'Dan White? The American architect?'

'Yes.'

'Why? What's in it for you?'

He laughed once, spread his hands. 'Nothing.'

Lizzie was silent for a moment. 'Then what's going on, Cormac? Who are you *playing* now? Me?' She put her hands on her hips, despair giving way to anger. 'Are you spinning me some story because you need me once more? Is Jan waiting outside for our happy reunion? Or maybe it's someone else who needs proof of our wedded bliss. Stears? Your office? All of Edinburgh?' Her voice rose in a shriek. '*What?* What do you want from me now?'

Cormac stood up. His eyes were as bright as a flame and his gaze went straight into her, searing her soul. 'I want you.'

She shook her head. 'No…'

'I know, it's hard to believe. I have no right to expect you to believe me, Lizzie, because I've lied and cheated my way here. But here—now—is the truth. I love you.'

'You're just saying it…'

'And meaning it.'

'No…'

'Yes. You've shown me what love is, Lizzie. You lived it. You gave yourself to me—to your sister—without ever expecting anything back. I convinced myself you were using me, as I was using you, but neither was the case. I fell in love with you a while back, Lizzie, in Sint Rimbert. I thought I could intimidate and control you, but you proved me wrong again and again. You controlled *me*.'

'This isn't about control…'

'No, it isn't. It's hard for me to understand that, even now. I don't know what love is. I realise that. Last night I refused to believe that I loved you. I didn't think you could love me. Not the real me. Not if you really knew me. And I didn't want you to be disappointed in me…or to be disappointed myself. Hurt.' He swallowed. 'So I said we were finished, because I believed that was all we could have. A night. But then tonight, when you got up from that table, I realised I couldn't let you go. I had to tell you the truth…except I don't know how, I'm making a mess of it, because I never have before.' He took a step towards her, his hands extended towards her, palms upwards in appeal. '*Show me.*'

She gave a laugh that trembled on the air. 'I'm not sure I can.'

'Then let me try.' Cormac gazed at her steadily, his hands spread wide. 'Lizzie, I love you.'

She took a step towards him, her voice a breath. 'Are you playing a game?' she whispered and in that question was all the fear, all the need, and all the hope.

'I'm giving you my heart.'

She shook her head. It was too wonderful, too easy. She couldn't quite believe it, as much as she wanted to.

She took a step back. 'Cormac…'

'You don't believe me.' He spoke calmly and a light of determination blazed in his eyes.

'I don't know what to believe. Everything has been false.'

'Not everything,' he corrected quietly.

'Tell me, then. When have you not been using me? When you tricked me on the plane?'

'I was using you then.'

'When you kissed me in the garden? When you suggested we have an affair?'

'Yes, then, too.' His voice was steady, but she thought she saw regret shadow his eyes.

'On the beach? At the villa? All those kind words, the understanding?'

'Yes. Then.'

She'd known as much, but it still hurt.

'The whole time.'

'Pretty much.' He smiled bleakly. 'I know you have no reason to believe me now. And even if you did, maybe you can't forgive me. I used you, Lizzie, and I didn't even feel guilty about it. I didn't know how. But you woke me up, something inside me I thought was dead. At first I thought it was just my conscience, but now I know it was my heart.'

'And now?'

'Now I feel like I'm dying inside.' He shrugged. 'It's not a particularly nice feeling.'

'No,' Lizzie agreed, 'it's not.'

'Then…' He paused. Waited.

She shook her head. She still couldn't believe. Wouldn't let herself. He'd played her too many times, had said the things she wanted to hear without meaning a word. 'When you stumbled in your presentation, were you doing that to gain Jan's sympathy?' she asked. 'To make him think you cared for me?'

'No.' Cormac shook his head. 'I said that because I couldn't admit the truth, not even to myself. It was what Jan had said. "This resort means everything to you." And I realised it did, and it wasn't enough. It was empty. Then he said I could bring my own family back, and the only person I thought of who remotely fitted that description was—you.' He gave a crooked smile. 'That terrified me.'

'Cormac!' Her voice was a choked plea. 'If you're lying now, for whatever reason…'

'This is the truth.'

'But you were going to use me, in Strathairn. Seduce me, tell me you loved me, even after you'd felt that? Realised that?' She laughed, a jagged sound of desperation. 'That was *yesterday*.'

'It was tearing me apart,' Cormac confessed quietly. 'I didn't want to do it, but I didn't think there was any other choice. I didn't know of any other choice. I've never felt I had any.'

'And that's not what you did?' Lizzie dragged in a breath. 'At the house…all those things you said…that wasn't just another tactic? Another ploy?'

His eyes widened. 'No, Lizzie. *No*. That was the truth. That was *me*. That was what was so amazing, so wonderful…that I told you, I showed you who I really was, and you wanted me. You wanted me.'

'Yes,' she admitted in a raw whisper. 'I did.' *I do.*

'Lizzie, I love you. I love you.'

She wanted to believe so much. So much. Yet still, she was afraid. So afraid. 'Cormac, I don't… I can't…'

'I understand.' He nodded. 'I could hardly expect you to… I can give you time. To think. Just don't…don't say never. Not yet.'

'Not yet,' Lizzie agreed, her throat, her heart, every part of her aching.

With a nod of resolute acceptance, Cormac turned and walked out of the house, into the darkness.

She didn't sleep that night. She lay in bed, dry-eyed, heart whirling, wondering, wanting to believe.

Her mind combed over the last week, the last day, the last *hour*, and sought answers.

Sought hope.

As dawn crawled over the grey horizon, pale, weak rays of light barely breaking through the heavy clouds, Lizzie knew her answer.

She knew her heart.

She loved Cormac, and love trusted. Love believed.

She felt lighter, even though her mind still seethed with worry, with fear, as she walked to the office that morning.

She ignored the speculative looks of the staff, knew everyone had heard the gossip and she didn't care.

Cormac, she saw to her disappointment, wasn't there. He'd left a note on her desk explaining that he would be out till the late afternoon. She read the postscript: *I wanted to give you time.*

She couldn't work, couldn't even think. She just wanted to see him, feel him, tell him.

The morning was spent in anxious silence, and when the phone rang after lunch she grabbed it.

'Yes?'

'Elizabeth? It's Jan Hassell.'

'Jan.' Her throat was suddenly dry, her hand slippery on the phone. 'I'm sorry for my behaviour last night. I trust Cormac explained…'

'Yes, he did. Don't worry, I know how it is with young couples. You are still working so much out.'

She frowned. 'Yes…'

'I only wanted to congratulate Cormac on the commission once again. We're hoping to have the two of you to Sint Rimbert for the ground breaking in the near future. The contract should be there by courier this afternoon. Once it's signed, you two should celebrate!'

'Celebrate,' Lizzie repeated, her mind numb. Her heart numb. 'Yes. We'll do that.' Somehow she managed to exchange pleasantries with Jan for a few minutes, even though she felt frozen: her body's—her heart's—way of coping with the pain. The knowledge.

He'd lied. Again. Everything must have been a lie—*everything*. Every carefully considered word he'd said last night, when he'd told her he loved her, needed her…

Why else would Jan still think they were married? Why would he be granting Cormac the commission?

Why had Cormac lied?

It must have been the only way to make Jan believe they were still a couple, she realised dully. And, of course, she had to believe it, too. He'd wanted to convince Jan that even though he'd lied at the beginning, he wasn't lying now.

Except he was.

He *was*.

Just as he'd been at every other point she'd stupidly convinced herself was real.

Nothing was real.

Not their first kiss, not their shared night. Not now.

Nothing.

She laid her head on her arms, every inch of her aching.

The contract arrived by courier; Lizzie signed for it with a heavy heart. It was easier to blunt the pain than to feel so very much.

Cormac came in just as the sun was setting, casting long shadows across the floor. Lizzie sat at her desk, staring blindly, blankly at the computer screen.

He knew at once that something was wrong; she could tell by his voice. 'Lizzie…' he asked cautiously, and she looked up at him with bleak eyes.

'Jan rang.'

'Did he?' He spoke neutrally, ominously so.

'He was very understanding, as you said before.' Her voice was brittle. She *felt* brittle, fragile, ready to splinter apart into jagged pieces. 'He seemed to think we were still married. He was still planning on giving you the commission. In fact…' her voice rose as she brandished the envelope she'd signed for '…here it is.'

'So I see.' He was still, tense, his eyes dark. She had no idea what he was thinking, what he'd do, what he'd done. She wanted him to deny it, to tell her again that he loved her…

It wasn't going to happen.

He'd got what he wanted. From her.

'So you did it, Cormac,' she continued in a high, false voice. 'You got your commission. Congratulations.'

'Thank you.' He spoke flatly, his face and tone dispassionate, and it carved great jagged pieces out of Lizzie's heart as every suspicion, every fear was confirmed with cruel clarity.

'So that's it, then. You don't need me any more. My *usefulness* is over.' She glanced at him; his face was as blank and as hard as stone.

'I don't need you for the commission, no.'

She nodded, stood up on trembling legs. 'So should I just go? You can send me the cheque.'

'Is that what you want?' His tone was almost indifferent and it cut her to the bone.

She tried to laugh; it came out as a sob. 'What do you think?'

He shrugged. 'You asked for time; I gave it to you. This seems to be your decision.'

She stared at him, incredulous. '*My* decision? What about *your* decision—to lie to me again and again? All I want to know is why, Cormac. Why did you lie to me last night? Why bother telling me you loved me? Jan had obviously already believed your performance. You didn't need to. Or was it just insurance? Or just…' her breath caught on a ragged sob '…because that's the only way you know how to be with me? With anyone?'

She looked down, choking back another sob, and wiped her eyes with her fists.

'I didn't lie.'

'What?' She looked up, blinked back more tears.

'I didn't lie,' Cormac repeated. 'I told you the truth last night. But there's nothing I can do to make you believe me, is there? Because you know the kind of man I am. The man I was.'

'You love me?' Lizzie repeated in disbelief.

'Yes. Well…' he paused, smiled crookedly '…I love the woman who believed in me, in a part of me I didn't know existed. A woman who showed me what kindness and goodness really are, who saw it in me and allowed me to see it in myself. I love her because she first loved me.'

Lizzie shook her head slowly. 'But…'

'Lizzie, I don't know what Jan told you.' He braced his hands on her desk. 'I don't know why he thinks we're still married. I let him know we were a couple, because I *believed* in that. I believed in us. It felt like the only thing saving me.'

'He did say "couple",' Lizzie admitted slowly. 'But…'

'I don't know why he's changed his mind and granted me the commission,' Cormac continued. 'And I don't care. I won't accept it.' He grabbed the envelope, tore it open and took out the coveted contract. Lizzie watched while he ripped it in half. 'I don't care! Do you want me to announce to the press, to the world, that I faked our marriage? I'll do it. Tell me what you want me to do.'

'Not that,' Lizzie whispered, shaken.

'I love you. *I love you*.' He stood there, helpless, a man who was used to knowing what to do, used to taking control. Now at her mercy, by his own volition. His own will.

He strode into his office and yanked several drawers of his desk open before he came back brandishing his sketchbook. 'You know what this is?'

She shook her head. 'Designs…'

'Sketches. Of you.' He tossed the book on her desk; it fell open

to a drawing of her. Asleep. She lay in a bed—their bed on Sint
Rimbert—one curled hand by her head, her hair tangled on the
pillow.

She gazed down at the picture, turned the page and saw
another sketch of her. And another. All drawn with loving care,
each one capturing a different pose, a different mood.

'I had to draw you. I didn't know why; I thought it was just
a passing fancy—I convinced myself. But it was more,' Cormac
confessed in a hoarse voice. 'Drawing—sketching—has always
been my secret passion. The one thing I felt I really cared about.'

'What about buildings?'

'They were drawings, too, of a different sort.' He paused.
'Look at the first sketch I did of you.'

She riffled through the pages and saw the sketch. It had been
done in the airport. She was sitting in a leather chair, looking
pensive and a bit worried. She looked up.

'Even then?' she whispered, her throat raw and aching.

'Even then. Though I didn't know it.' He turned to her, his
hands spread. 'Lizzie, I don't know what to do. Show me.'

She closed the book and looked up. 'Cormac…'

'Yes.' He gazed at her and his heart was in his eyes. So was
hers.

'I love you.'

He closed his eyes briefly. 'Thank God.' He moved to her,
pulled her into his arms and rested his chin on her hair. *'Thank
God.'*

'I'm sorry I didn't believe you,' Lizzie whispered.

'No. No, you are not the one to be sorry. I'm sorry for deceiving you—and myself—for so long. I should have…'

'It doesn't matter.'

Her arms were around him, holding him tight. He tilted her
chin up so their eyes met.

'Will you marry me? For real? For ever?'

'Yes.' She nodded, wondering why she was still crying when
she felt so happy. So blessed.

'I still don't know how to love. I'll make mistakes. I'll forget.
I'll…'

'I'll show you,' Lizzie promised, and began to do just that.

EPILOGUE

Two years later

SUNSHINE poured through the windows and a balmy tropical breeze caused a shutter to bang as Lizzie dozed in bed. From her bedside she heard a faint mewling noise and she stirred sleepily.

'Someone's hungry.' Cormac came into the room, scooping his daughter from the bassinet with newly expert arms.

'She just ate.' Lizzie laughed, but she scooted into a sitting position while Cormac handed her Emily Douglas, their two-month-old daughter.

'Have I missed anything terribly important?' she asked as she put Emily to her breast.

'Just more receptions and handshaking.' Cormac sat on the edge of the bed, a faint smile on his face as he watched her nurse their child.

The resort at Sint Rimbert had officially opened two days ago and Lizzie had been insistent that they take their family for the opening ceremony. Dan White, the co-architect, Wendy and their toddler, Stephen, had also come.

'The press *has* been euphoric,' Lizzie said with a little smile. '"The most innovative collaboration in years,"' she quoted.

'Yes,' Cormac agreed, smiling wryly, 'I don't think they could believe that someone like me could actually collaborate with any-one.'

'Wonders never cease,' Lizzie teased.

'No,' Cormac agreed, 'they don't.'

Lizzie never tired of these shared moments. They were still new, still precious, still filled with joy.

She knew they always would be.

The last six weeks had been a haze of both fatigue and joy. Dani, having started a new course at a different university, was a doting aunt, and Cormac couldn't get enough of his new daughter…his new family.

The success of the resort was a bonus added to an already overflowing cup of blessing.

Just then Emily wrenched away from Lizzie's breast and gave a loud satisfied burp.

Lizzie looked up and grinned. 'She has a lusty appetite.'

'So do I.' Cormac grinned back, then stroked Emily's downy head. 'We're blessed, aren't we?' he asked softly. 'To have all this.'

Lizzie nodded, a lump in her throat. 'I never thought I'd have a family again.'

'And I never thought I'd have one at all.' He smiled. 'Come here, poppet. Time for a nappy change.'

Lizzie sat back, watched as Cormac fiddled helplessly with the tiny nappy. The baby set to bawling.

'Look,' she said, exasperated, 'there are sticky tabs! You've got it on backwards!'

She strode over, laughing, and he gave a shamefaced grin.

She paused, eyes narrowed. 'You're not *pretending* to not know how, are you?' she asked.

Cormac hung his head. 'Who, me?' His eyes glinted with humour and something infinitely more precious. Something real. 'Why don't you show me?'

'I have to show you everything, don't I?'

'Yes,' Cormac replied seriously. 'You do.' He fiddled with the nappy, finally managed to get it on. 'There. See? I'm a quick learner.'

'Yes,' Lizzie agreed as he pulled her in for a kiss, their daughter cradled in one strong arm, 'you certainly are.'